The Price of Desire

By Leda Swann

THE PRICE OF DESIRE
SUGAR AND SPICE

LEDA SWANN

The Price of Desire

An Imprint of HarperCollins*Publishers*
www.harpercollins.com

This is a work of fiction. Names, characters, places, and incidents are products of the author's imagination or are used fictitiously and are not to be construed as real. Any resemblance to actual events, locales, organizations, or persons, living or dead, is entirely coincidental.

THE PRICE OF DESIRE. Copyright © 2007 by Leda Swann. All rights reserved. Printed in the United States of America. No part of this book may be used or reproduced in any manner whatsoever without written permission except in the case of brief quotations embodied in critical articles and reviews. For information address HarperCollins Publishers, 10 East 53rd Street, New York, NY 10022.

HarperCollins books may be purchased for educational, business, or sales promotional use. For information please write: Special Markets Department, HarperCollins Publishers, 10 East 53rd Street, New York, NY 10022.

FIRST EDITION

Interior text designed by Diahann Sturge

Library of Congress Cataloging-in-Publication Data

Swann, Leda.
　The price of desire / by Leda Swann.—1st ed.
　　p.　cm.
ISBN: 978-0-06-117644-9
ISBN-10: 0-06-117644-3
I. Title.

PS3619.I548P75　2007
813'.6—dc22　　　　　　　2006018493

07　08　09　10　11　RRD　10　9　8　7　6　5　4　3　2　1

One

Caroline Clemens pasted a smile on her face as she gazed belligerently over the assembled company.

Her insides cramped with fear, but she did not let her discomfort show on her face. At any sign of weakness, the pack would race in for the kill. They did not deserve the satisfaction of watching her crumble. She would outface all the malicious gossip from those old spinsters who had always envied her, and all the false condolences from pretend friends who had come to crow over her misfortune.

Heaven help her, but tonight she could even bear the unfeigned sympathy of the handful of people who genuinely loved her.

She cast her eyes over the sea of color in front of her, looking for the red and gold jacket of Captain Bellamy. He, at least, loved her well. The small matter of her family's bankruptcy would not matter to him a whit. Only last week, when the rumors of her family's financial troubles were starting to make the rounds, he had sworn to her that he would love her even if she were a pauper.

The Captain's earnestness had made her smile at the time, but she clung wistfully to the memory now. Last week she had known only that she could not afford the new pair of kid gloves she needed, even though her old ones were worn and stained. Tonight she knew the whole nasty truth. Her entire family was ruined. Utterly and irretrievably ruined.

At the end of the month their house in Mayfair and all their household effects would go under the hammer. Her father's untimely death had made absolutely sure that nothing would be left for them to live on. Nothing.

Were it not for her impending marriage to Captain Bellamy, she and her younger sisters and brother would be facing the workhouse. She shuddered. There was no point in dwelling on the horrors of the workhouse—the rough clothes, the hard labor, the poor food that scarcely kept body and soul together, and the disease that carried you off in the end if starvation and exhaustion didn't claim you first. The Captain would save her from that. He would save all of them.

As she scanned the crowd looking for her savior, her gaze was arrested by that of another man. He was a stranger to her, which in itself was enough to catch her attention. Few strangers successfully braved the close-knit society of London merchant bankers to which her family belonged. Though they took carefully calculated risks in their business dealings, when it came to making acquaintances for their wives and daughters, they eliminated any chance of risk. Only the most impeccably respectable personages were ever allowed to visit or to mingle with them in their infrequent evening soirees.

Caroline allowed herself a wry smile. No doubt those same impeccable personages were now watching avidly from the sidelines, salivating at the thought of ripping her to shreds.

The stranger caught her smile and evidently thought it was meant for him. He raised his eyebrows at her in a friendly if somewhat surprised acknowledgment and returned her smile with one of his own.

Caroline caught her breath at the sight. His smile transformed his face from that of an eminently respectable personage into an enticement to sin. Devilry danced in his eyes, promising delights that she had never dreamed of. His face, tanned a deep brown by the sun, no longer looked weatherbeaten and oddly out of place in an English autumn, but somehow full of dangerously alluring mystery.

He stepped forward as if to claim the right to make her acquaintance. Though his figure was stolidly dressed in a dark suit similar to those worn by nearly every other man in the room, underneath the drab clothes he moved sinuously, gracefully, with the barely controlled energy of a panther. He radiated an energy too powerful to stop, wrapped in a gorgeous pelt that begged to be touched despite the obvious danger.

What caught her most about him, though, were his eyes. They hypnotized her; she could not look away. With deliberate focus he held her gaze with his, not allowing her any chance to move away as he came toward her.

"We have met before?" His voice was warm and deep, and it enveloped her in its richness. Though his diction was perfect, his accent was unusually soft and burred, and it fell on her ears like a caress.

She shook her head, still unable to look away from the deep brown of his eyes. "I do not believe so," she replied, her mouth so dry it was difficult to speak.

"Then allow me to introduce myself."

She inclined her head slightly. His presence acted like a powerful drug on her. Even if she had wanted to refuse his acquaintance, she was unable to deny him anything. His inexplicable power over her was too strong to resist.

He bowed low over her hand. "Dominic Savage at your service."

Her tongue sneaked out to lick her bottom lip as he bowed over her hand. He caught the movement and his smile grew fractionally wider.

"Caroline. C-Caroline Clemens," she replied, giving him her full name without a thought. His effect on her senses demanded such a familiarity.

His eyes narrowed. "You are related to Isaac Clemens, then? The Clemens who recently—"

Anger clutched at her soul at the look of distaste that flashed over his face, though she could not break the spell he cast over her. "Yes, I am," she broke in coldly, knowing what he was about to say. Her father's misfortunes would have been whispered into his ear by any number of gossips by now, but she had not thought anyone could be so ill-mannered as to mention it to her face.

"I see."

The sudden veiling of his eyes finally allowed her to break away from his gaze. Moving her head almost imperceptibly to the side, she removed herself from any danger of being caught in the grip of his inescapable stare. Whatever strange power he wielded over her, she would not be tricked by it a second time. She would never dare to look directly into his face again.

Ah, there was the Captain in the far corner, talking animatedly to Kitty Earnshaw, his bright red jacket standing out from the crowd of black and white. The sight of him was like a breath of fresh country air on a mind clouded with heavily spiced and perfumed incense. She could think clearly once more.

"If you will excuse me," she said regally to Mr. Savage, inclining her head in polite dismissal. Now that he had learned her name and recognized her as a pariah within this circle of successful bankers and businessmen, no doubt he would be glad to see the back of her. He would not choose to further the acquaintance he had made on a whim.

Neither did she choose to associate with someone so clearly ill-bred. Judged on his manners alone, he was no better than his name—a savage by both name and by nature.

"I'd rather not."

She blinked, arrested in the middle of gliding away. "I beg your pardon? Is there something wrong?"

"I'd rather not excuse you just yet. I was hoping to talk to you."

She risked a sidelong glance at him. His look of distaste was gone, replaced by a curious interest. "What do you want to say to me?"

"You are a beautiful woman and I am a stranger here in London. Is it any wonder that I should like to pass a pleasant evening talking to you?"

Nothing could have marked him out as a stranger more clearly than his overfriendly attitude toward a bankrupt's daughter. "Even though you know who I am?" Did he not know that the taint of her family's misfortune spoiled everything it touched?

"Especially then." He placed her hand in the crook of his arm. "Come, talk with me. Entertain me on this dull evening."

The touch of his arm under her gloved hand sent rivers of fire through her body. "I fear I am a dull companion tonight." She had to go talk to the Captain, not waste her precious evening with a strange man who made her bones melt.

"Let me entertain you, then." His voice was a caress, the low tones making her intimate parts prickle with awareness. "I have been away from England far too long and I am starved of the company of Englishwomen."

She was in no mood to pander to the curiosity of a stranger, or to provide him with the entertainment he was seeking. Besides, the effect he had on her was too unsettling. "I doubt you would have anything to say that I would wish to hear," she said in her most repressive tone.

Her coldness just made him grin at her. "Should you not listen to me first before you judge?"

"I do not have to listen to the Devil to know that he lies." She tried to move away but he held her hand in his so she could not escape.

"Touché." His sudden burst of laughter caught her by surprise. "Though I do not think it very polite of you to liken me to such an old reprobate. All I wanted was to tell you what a beautiful woman you are, how your eyes shine as green as emeralds, and your skin gleams soft in the gaslight."

No honest man would pay her such extravagant compliments. "If the cap fits ..." Her words trailed off into an insulting silence, and she took advantage of the moment to look around surreptitiously for the Captain. *He* was an honest man and would never tell her that her eyes were as green as emeralds, or clasp her hand to his in an improper fashion.

There he was, still closeted in the corner with Kitty. Unusually, he had not yet noticed her presence among the guests and rushed to her side.

"Who are you looking for so assiduously?" Mr. Savage inquired. "Has your lover misplaced himself?" He followed the line of her gaze. "Ah, the handsome Captain in his regimentals is worshipping at another shrine? Is that what is making you so abrupt?"

"He is not—I mean, I am not—oh, forget I ever spoke," she snapped.

"He's no great loss—up to his ears in debt and hanging out for a rich wife, by all accounts. A woman like yourself could do far better."

His rudeness was matched only by his arrogance and ignorance. "You, for example?" she asked, raising her eyebrows at him in a gesture of disbelief.

"Naturally. I would be happy to stand in the Captain's place." He reached out and stroked her cheek lightly with the tips of his fingers. "He will use his aristocratic connections to snare his wealthy wife and will have no time left over for you. You will sleep alone in your bed every night waiting for him to come to you, to stroke your fine white skin and to love your beautiful body."

The touch of his hand on her face shocked her with its intimacy, yet she could not draw away.

"I would not leave you alone in your bed for a single night if you were mine. I would run my fingers through your hair and caress your soft skin, delving into your most secret places. Not an inch of you would be a secret to me, or remain unexplored by my hands, my mouth, my tongue. Every part of you would be open to me, wet and wild with wanting me. And I would keep you that way every night."

His fingers, rough and callused from heavy work, were cool

against her cheek. She clamped her legs together to stop them from trembling, unable to summon the necessary words to correct his misapprehension. The Captain was not her lover, but her affianced husband. She would be the wife he would lay beside at night, the woman he would turn to and take gently in his arms—

She stopped her thoughts in their tracks. Her lack of experience meant that not even her imagination could take her any further.

"You deserve a better man than the Captain to warm your bed at night. You deserve a man who is generous in all ways, with his money and his time and his affection. You need a man who cares for your pleasure more than he cares for his own to keep you satisfied." His eyes bored into hers, robbing her of the power to speak. "Is the Captain a man like that? Does he see to your pleasure, or does he rut on top of you like a beast, caring only for himself, prizing you only as a vessel in which to spend his seed?"

His fingertips were on her neck now, raising goose bumps wherever they touched her. She could not shake them away, though whether it was a failure of her will or her body, she could not say. All she knew was that she was caught in his net again, unable to move.

"Does he kiss your white breasts and suckle on your nipples until they tighten into hard nubs under him?" His breath was hot on her neck and his questions the merest whisper of sound in her ear. "Does he stroke your soft pussy with his fingers and watch you writhe in an agony of wanting? Does he caress you with his tongue until you scream with pleasure under him? Then when you are molten with desire, does he fuck you hard and fast like I would fuck you, thrusting my cock into your cunt over and over again until you explode with a woman's pleasure?"

His last, most shocking words finally broke her free of his spell. "The Captain is a finer man than twenty of you together," she spat at him, drawing back from his touch as if it stung her. "You are a filthy lecher and you disgust me." How lowly he must think of her to whisper such words in her ear. He had to be the worst sort of scoundrel to proposition her so baldly in such respectable company.

To her surprise, he gave a bark of laughter. "You are priceless. You look as sweet and mild as a kitten, but under that veneer of softness you are all teeth and claws. Tell me, are all Englishwomen such spitfires when a man whispers words of love into their ears?"

Words of love? She snorted. Mr. Savage did not know what real love was. Love was tender respect and gentle gallantry, not whispered suggestions of lust and deviancy. "I am hardly in a position to judge the temper of Englishwomen. I do not make a practice of insulting them." She inclined her head in the barest nod and jerked her arm away from him. "Now, if you will excuse me, the Captain will be waiting for me." And she walked steadily away without stopping for an answer.

The sound of a chuckle followed her. "It was my pleasure

meeting you, sweet Caroline. Just remember me when the Captain casts you aside. I will be waiting for you."

Worshipping at another shrine? Out to snare a wealthy wife? Planning to cast her aside? Mr. Savage's casual judgment had aimed a shaft of fear straight at her breast.

Would the Captain abandon her now, just when she needed him most? Even though they were contracted in a solemn and binding vow? She did not like to think so. Indeed, she did not *dare* to think so, for if he failed her, she and all her family were lost.

The walk across the crowded room seemed an eternity to her. Little had the Captain known of the burden he would have to shoulder when he asked for her hand in marriage three long months ago. Was he now regretting his request?

She had liked him well enough, and not preferred any other man, but had accepted his suit mostly because her father had pressed it on her. The Captain's staunch support of her in her time of need, however, had added gratitude to her feelings for him, and caused liking to blossom into love. He was a worthy man, and she would endeavor to deserve his goodness for as long as she lived.

Her head held high, she made her way through the crowd toward him. She did not have the patience to wait for him to notice she had arrived and to come to her rescue. Her pride was already stretched to the limits of her endurance; her soul was hurting, and his embrace was her harbor against the storm.

People parted in front of her as if she carried the seeds of contagion with her. Nobody wanted to touch her and risk the taint of her family's bankruptcy. Isolated in the middle of a crowd, she felt like a leper with a silent bell, warning others to keep their distance from her and to avoid her fate.

Kitty Earnshaw looked up as Caroline approached them. Her face colored an unbecoming shade of pink and she tugged uncomfortably at one of the pale brown ringlets that framed her face. Unable to meet Caroline's eyes, she dropped her gaze to the floor.

Captain Bellamy turned and graced Caroline with a smile. "Miss Clemens."

Was it her imagination or did his eyes look shifty, as if he, too, found it hard to meet her gaze?

Silently chiding herself, she took his proffered arm with gratitude. Her own misfortunes were causing her to see trouble everywhere, even where it did not exist. "If you will excuse us," she said to Kitty, "the Captain and I would like to take a turn about the room."

Kitty had already backed away and was cowering in the corner. At Caroline's polite dismissal, she scurried off, clearly not wishing to be involved in a confrontation.

"I gather you have something specifically to say to me," the Captain said in a low tone as they walked arm in arm through the room. "I presume that was your intention in frightening away poor Kitty Earnshaw. Or are you simply suffering from a fit of womanish vapors brought on by seeing me conversing with another young woman?"

"I did not frighten her away," Caroline protested. The hint of unkindness in his voice disturbed her greatly. He had always appeared to be the perfect gentleman—gentle, tender, and forbearing with all her many faults.

"You did bear down on her looking more than commonly haughty and displeased. It was no wonder the poor girl could hardly speak for fright when she saw you coming. Though I'm sure you did not mean to scare her," he added somewhat as an afterthought. "After all, what threat could she pose to you?"

Caroline gritted her teeth. "And nor do I suffer from womanish vapors."

He raised one eyebrow at her tone. "I am sure you do not."

His tone was so patently insincere that she clenched her teeth together tightly to prevent herself from speaking. There was nothing to be gained from a quarrel with him now. However dearly she wanted to complain at his lofty attitude, she knew she could not afford to.

Three months ago she had been a princess, today she was a pauper and reliant on the Captain's generosity. That alone must excuse his lack of gallantry, if he *was* lacking in such a commodity.

With a gentle pressure on his arm, she steered him toward the French doors that opened onto the balcony.

It had rained that morning, washing the air clean of the smuts and soot that had poisoned London's muggy summer air. The breeze was sweet with the rich scent of early autumn and the heady perfume of the late flowering tea roses.

On such a night like this, with the Captain at her side, she could almost forget her troubles.

His voice broke into her thoughts. "You are in full mourning, I see."

His tone of superiority irked her. He had not spoken to her like that before, or if he had, she'd never noticed it. Had he changed, or had she? "My father is dead," she reminded him curtly. "You would hardly expect me to be cavorting around in a yellow gown and ribbons when he is scarce buried."

"But such deep mourning? Under the circumstances, I do not think it is quite, uh ... proper. You ought at the most to be in gray or lavender."

Her fists were clenched so tightly at her sides that her fingernails almost drew blood. "My father is dead. No matter how he died." Wearing deep black was a mark of respect for her father's memory that she would not forgo. Indeed, she had gravely depleted her store of ready money to fit herself and her sisters and brother out in suitable mourning clothes.

"I do not like it, Miss Clemens." His face was severe. "It is not fitting."

"I know that we cannot marry while I am still in full mourning," she said, making a stab at the cause of his irritation. "But a quiet ceremony at the end of six weeks would still be possible." She was reasonably confident that she could keep her siblings fed and housed until then, even though it would mean calling in every favor from every one of her friends. "My father's death need not alter our wedding plans too greatly."

The Captain did not reply at once. He was staring out over the garden, his hands gripping the rail of the balcony so tightly that his knuckles gleamed white in the evening gloom.

The tense look on his face sent tendrils of fear snaking up her spine. "William?" she said softly, desperately, placing one of her hands on his, claiming him as was her right. She could not let him desert her now.

He turned his head away from her pleading. "I cannot marry you," he said baldly.

His words were soft but lethal. Only her pride kept her from sinking to the ground in despair. With that one breath, he consigned her and her family to the living death of the workhouse.

"While there was still the hope of some money coming to you from your father's estate, even though it was far less than the fifty thousand pounds your father and I had settled on as your dowry, I was willing to honor our agreement." He ran one hand through his hair. "I love you, Caroline. I love you enough to take you for only twenty thousand pounds, or even ten thousand. I would have been content with only ten."

The light of understanding began to dawn on her, and a dim, dreary light it was. "But there is nothing left for my dowry. Worse than nothing. Papa left debts I can never hope to pay."

He turned to face her, his eyes haunted. "Caroline, I do love you."

What use did she have for such a lukewarm love? She would

rather have his hatred than such a conditional affection as he offered her. "Just not enough to marry me now that I am a pauper."

"I cannot afford to take you as my wife. I am far from rich, as your father knew well. I need a woman who will add to my wealth, not be a drain on it."

"You are breaking our engagement, then?" A brittle laugh escaped her. "How will you find another wife when your behavior toward me becomes known? A gentleman never breaks his word to a lady."

"You are right—I cannot break it."

He turned toward her, but the shaft of hope starting to rise in her was quickly dispelled by his next words.

"I need you to break it. I need you to offer to release me from our engagement, an offer that I will then regretfully accept."

"You want me to cut my own lifeline? The only hope that my family has of regaining respectability?" Was he so cruel as to put a knife in her hand and tell her that she must die, and then ask her to stab herself because he had not the heart to kill her outright? "I cannot do it. You should not ask it of me."

"I can make it worth your while."

"You would pay to get rid of me?" Given that she could force him to honor his engagement or have him publicly labeled as an untrustworthy rogue, she should not be surprised that in his eyes he owed her some compensation. No budding businessman could survive the blackening of his reputation.

It was a sign of her desperation that she would even listen to such an outrageous proposal, let alone consider accepting money from him, but the prospect of her sisters and brother in the workhouse forced her hand. "How much?"

"If you release me, I have Mr. Earnshaw's permission to seek the hand of his daughter, Kitty." His face relaxed into a self-satisfied smile. "The girl does not seem averse to the match. All going well, I will wed her within the fortnight."

"Mr. Earnshaw is a wealthy man. Wealthier than Papa was, even before..."

"She comes with sixty thousand pounds in the hand, and a half share in the business when Mr. Earnshaw passes away."

And she came with nothing. With less than nothing, seeing she had four sisters and a brother to support as well. Such a sum as Kitty had for a dowry would be no small temptation even to a greater man than the Captain. No wonder he was so ready to throw her over for another girl.

"While you still had hopes of a dowry, there was no reason for me to look twice at Kitty Earnshaw. Though she seems quiet and amenable enough, she is not half as pretty or as spirited as you are. But now you have none..." He spread his hands wide in a gesture of helplessness. "You must understand my situation."

She did not care to understand him further. All that mattered to her now was that he would pay her a goodly amount so he could wed Kitty's dowry. "What will you pay me to break our engagement?" Her voice came out hard.

"When Kitty and I are wed, I will pay the rent on a modest house in town for you, and add an annuity of two hundred pounds a year ..."

A rent-free cottage and two hundred pounds a year would be barely enough for all five of them to scrape by on, but with a little bit of luck, it would be enough. Though it was by no means generous, the sum would at least keep them out of the workhouse. She felt no guilt in accepting it. It was little enough for him to pay to exchange a poor fiancée for a rich one.

"... an extra payment of five hundred pounds for every child you bear me, and a reduced annuity of fifty pounds a year if ever our liaison should come to an end."

She'd been so fixated on the tantalizing prospect of a modest competency to support her family that she almost missed the end of his proposal. Her eyes widened in horror as the realization of what he was offering her struck home. "You are offering to become my keeper? You want me to be your whore?"

A black cloud of despair descended over her. He was asking her to release him from their engagement and to become his mistress instead. For two hundred pounds a year. Such a sum would scarce keep her and her family in coal over the winter. The offer which half a minute ago had seemed tolerable enough was now exposed as hopelessly and insultingly mean and penny-pinching. "And what of poor Kitty? You would marry her though you do not love her enough to be faithful to her?"

If her father had been alive, the Captain would never have dared to make her such an offer. If only her father had not given up hope that his speculations would one day be success-ful. But he *had* given up hope. Last Thursday night in his study he had put a gun to his head and abandoned them all.

"Do not worry about Kitty." He brushed aside her fears with a wave of his hand. "I will be kind enough to the girl. She will have no cause to regret marrying me."

Though she had no reason to love Kitty, his callous dis-missal of his intended bride made her stomach roil with anger. "Even though you would use her money to set me up as your mistress?"

"I cannot marry you, but I still love you." His voice turned smooth and pleading, as if it were coated in cream. "Think about it, Caroline. If we were to marry, we would be poor to-gether. You are too fine a woman to live in poverty."

"I do not fear being poor." Poverty was manageable, toler-able even. She had already learned to live with it. Utter des-titution was what she really feared. The workhouse. It sent a shiver of fear snaking up her spine whenever she thought of it.

"Be sensible, Caroline, and look logically at the situation. My way we both get what we need. I can set myself up in busi-ness and still be with the woman I love, and you get to live a comfortable life with your family and still be with the man *you* love. For you *do* love me, don't you?"

For a horrible moment she wanted to accept. She wanted to be generous and allow him to be generous to her in return. Two hundred pounds a year was a goodly sum to a family that was facing the workhouse. Surely her father would have understood the dire straits that led her to take such a desperate path.

That much, at least, she knew was true. Her father would have understood and he would have forgiven her.

But her pride was stronger than her fear. She would not take the easy way out like her father had. He had spared himself the shame of his situation with a bullet to his brain, and left his family in double pain. Being the daughter of a bankrupt was shameful enough, but being the daughter of a failed banker who had committed suicide was worst of all. In escaping his troubles, he had doomed his family to a living hell.

She straightened her spine. Hard though it was, she would be stronger than her father. There would be no easy way out—not for her, nor for the Captain. He had made her a promise. Be it on his own head if he wanted to break it now. "No."

"No?"

"No, I will not become your mistress. Nor will I willingly release you from our engagement." Her voice was hard as stone. "If you no longer wish to marry me, if you intend to break your solemn vow to me, you will have to stand up like a man and take the consequences."

"Whether you release me or no, I will not marry you." His voice had turned low and menacing. "You cannot think to shame me into it. I will not condemn myself to a lifetime of poverty for fear of a moment of embarrassment."

"I know you will never marry me." She turned her back to him so he could not see the tears in her eyes. So much for her hopes and dreams of sharing her life with a man who loved her. The Captain had flung them to the ground and crushed them beneath the heel of his boots. "I am glad of it. After the offer you have made to me, I no longer want to marry you, either."

"Then why take this foolish road?" he entreated her, all honeyed warmth and gentle persuasion once more. "Be the woman that I know you are inside. Release me from my promise. It will cost you nothing and it will mean everything to me."

"You are asking me, a pauper, to give up everything I have left." Her soul felt like flint. There was not the slightest shred of mercy left in her. "You are asking me to give up my self-respect. I cannot do that. You should not ask it of me."

"I can make your life easier for you, or I can make it infinitely harder. The choice is yours."

"I do not fear your threats. They mean nothing to me."

He strode up and down along the balcony, his booted feet striking the stone flags forcefully. "You will live to regret your decision."

She would regret it more if she threw away her self-respect and became his mistress. "I do not care."

At her angry retort, his strides slowed. "You are over-wrought," he said, coming up behind her and putting his arms around her. His voice was low and gentle, as if she were a horse he needed to tame. "The shock of your father's death has been too much for your feminine sensibilities. I should not have as-saulted you with the full reality of the situation so soon."

Stiff and resisting, she suffered his embrace in silence. He had no right to touch her any longer.

"I will give you a fortnight to think it over and make your decision," he said, stroking her gently on one shoulder. "I could not, with any decency, announce my engagement to Kitty any earlier than that anyway."

His sudden change from threats to cajoling did not sway her. Her mind was made up. "You have my answer already. The passing of a fortnight will not change it."

He gave a quiet snigger that made her itch to slap him. "I will presume to hope that it will. You women are such vari-able creatures, prone to changing your minds on a whim, even when reason and logic have failed to sway you. Who knows what may happen in a fortnight to convince you?"

Leaning over her, he kissed the side of her neck with wet lips. "*Au revoir*, sweet Caroline. I will come to visit you Fri-day week in the hopes of finding you in a more amenable temper."

Not a muscle in her body moved as his military boots clat-tered over the stone flags back to the drawing room. Only when she heard the soft click of the door being latched behind him did she reach up to scrub the sensation of his kiss off her neck with her soiled kidskin gloves.

Her Captain had played her false. He had deserted her. Abandoned her. Now she was truly left without a hope of rescue.

With shaking legs she made her way to the edge of the terrace. She could not stay out here in the garden by herself, giving tacit acknowledgment to the severity of the blow he had just dealt her. Neither could she face returning to the drawing room just yet. Her soul revolted at the need to make polite conversation and pretend that nothing was amiss when her whole world had just shattered around her.

At the edge of the terrace stood a glass conservatory, the leaves of the lush plants inside gleaming eerily in the light of early evening. It beckoned her with the promise of temporary refuge.

Her skirts gathered in her hands, and her back as straight as she could make it, she walked carefully down the stone stairs of the terrace and through a side door into the conservatory.

Inside the misted glass walls the air was so heavy with the scent of hothouse flowers in bloom that she could hardly breathe. Water droplets hung suspended in the air, seeming to weep in company with her.

A wicker settee stood in one lonely corner, shaded with the large leaves of a drooping palm. Without a thought for the care of her sole black dress, she flung herself into it.

This last blow, so cruel and so unexpected, had utterly broken her. There was nothing left to live for, no hope of a better life for any of them.

She could not become the Captain's mistress, not when she had until so recently expected to become his wife. She would rather go on the streets and make her living on her back, letting strange men have their way with her in the dark night, than sell her body to the Captain for two hundred pounds a year. Nothing, not even the workhouse, could be so utterly demeaning as that.

As she sat there, despairing, it came to her that there was another way out—not just for her, but for all of them. A way out for her sisters and brother as well as herself. A way in which they could all escape, leaving none behind to mourn them.

The same way her father had taken.

If they were all to die, all of them, their troubles would be over and none would be left to carry the burden of grief and shame and loss.

The idea fluttered into her soul on poisoned wings that glittered as brightly as gold.

Her father's pistol was hidden away in his study on a high shelf. How many bullets remained in its chamber? Enough for her brother, her sisters, and then herself?

Now that the Captain had abandoned her, the six of them had nothing left but their pride, and that would not last long in the workhouse. Would it not be easier for them all if they were to die quickly instead of waiting for starvation and despair to kill them off by degrees? At least that way they would all die together, and none of them would have to suffer the grief of seeing their beloved siblings waste away in front of them.

She could surely harden her heart for long enough to send her brother and sisters to an everlasting sleep, where nothing would ever trouble them again. Life had nothing good to offer them. In death, they would all find peace.

Only a coward would hesitate with such a choice before her, and no one could call her a coward.

Her mind was made up. She would finish what her father had started. After tonight, the Clemens family would be no more.

This very evening, before she lost her nerve, she would do it. While they were sleeping, she would shoot them all, and then she would shoot herself.

Through the black despair that gripped her heart, she hesitated.

She did not want to die. There were so many things she still longed to do, so many things she had never done. She would never visit Paris in the springtime, or picnic in the woods at midnight with her lover. She would never ride in a hot air balloon, flying high above the ground as if she were a bird. She would never see her younger sisters well married or watch her brother Teddy grow to become a man.

But it was too late for her, too late for all of them. Her sisters would never marry and Teddy would be a boy forever. She would die tonight. She would die, and all her family with her.

As she rose from the chair and smoothed her dress, ready to brave the crows and take her last leave of all her friends and acquaintances, one last despairing regret went through her mind. *She would never make love to any man. She would die a virgin.*

Two

Dominic Savage leaned against the door frame, watching her.

She was brave, he'd give her that. There were no floods of tears, no hysterics—just that same icy calm demeanor as if nothing on this earth could touch her. He had to admire such self-possession, particularly in such a young woman. For all her self-control, she could not be much more than twenty.

Neither death nor desertion, it seemed, had the power to break her. Her heart was so well-guarded that not even losing her lover could penetrate it.

If she even had a heart.

Not that the Captain was worth crying about. He was clearly a man on the make, and he had a sure eye for the main chance. A poor widow of a bankrupt, even one as intriguing as Caroline Clemens, would never be able to keep the Captain's self-interested attentions for long.

Still, women were strange creatures and there was no accounting for a woman's taste in matters of the heart. She had probably fancied herself in love with him. "Being in love" was such a convenient justification for all kinds of selfish and self-indulgent behavior. It was certainly more than enough excuse for a very young woman married to a rather elderly and sober-natured gentleman to take herself a handsome young lover.

What would it take to overcome her defenses, to breach the wall that she had built around herself? What would make her face crumple into tears or her voice cry out in anguish? Neither husband nor lover had made her weep.

A flicker of movement from her still figure caught his attention. Her fists were clenched together so tightly that her knuckles blanched.

Interesting. She felt emotion keenly then, she just did not show it.

As he watched, she rose from the chair, her fists still clenching handfuls of her dress, and moved toward the door that led out into the garden. The soiree, for her at least, was clearly over.

No woman had intrigued him quite as much as Caroline Clemens did. Though she tried to hide her natural sensuality under layers of rigid self-control, every movement she made set his blood rushing into his groin. He wasn't ready to let her walk out of his life just yet. Moving forward, he blocked her exit. "Has your Captain deserted you already?"

She gave a start at the sound of his voice and turned toward him. "Ah, Mr. Savage. The man who entertains himself by mocking those less fortunate than himself. We meet again."

Though her speech was steady, the bitterness of her words and the wildness in her eyes startled him. She was far closer to the edge than he had at first thought. "I apologize," he said with all sincerity. "I did not intend to mock you."

She lifted one elegant eyebrow. "Indeed."

He had never met anyone who could do haughty and unconcerned as well as she could, even though her heart must be breaking inside. Try as she might to hide her hurt behind a facade of ice, now that he was close to her he could sense the pain she was concealing. The very air vibrated with it. "The Captain returned to the room some minutes before you did, looking out of humor. I came to search for you, thinking you must have quarreled."

Her eyebrow rose a fraction higher. "Your kindness to a stranger leaves me speechless." If her voice got any more tense, it would snap.

"You blame me for being pleased you are now free?" The closer he got to her, the hotter he could feel the fire that ran through her veins. Fire, wild and passionate, not the cold blue ice that she pretended to be.

He wanted her to feel his presence, to be attuned to him as he was to her. "I told you I would be waiting for you when you and the Captain parted company. And here I am, as promised. Just a little earlier than I expected."

She stiffened even further. "You are mistaken. The Captain and I have not quarreled."

She was lying. Her whole body, down to the way she carried herself so carefully and the brittle look in her eyes, told him so. He reached out and blotted a drop of water from her cheek with the pad of his thumb. "Then why do you look as if your whole world had fallen apart?"

She brushed him away with an impatient gesture. "That is not a tear. The air is damp in here from the ferns, that is all. I have not been crying." Her tone was fierce and brooked no denial.

"Look into my eyes, Caroline." He held her head gently so she could not avoid his command without twisting free. "You cannot think to lie to me. Not when the tear tracks still silver your cheeks."

"And what if I have been crying?" she asked, her voice almost savage, unable to look away from him. "Is it a crime? I thought myself alone in here. I *wished* myself to be alone." Her words were pointed barbs aimed at his breast.

He did not wound so easily. Her feeble weapons glanced off his tough hide and fell away to the ground. "I, too, wished you to be alone in here."

"So you could break into my solitude?"

"Exactly." He captured her gaze with his own, using all the force of his personality to hold her to him. "If you had not been alone, I could not have done what I intend to do."

Her teeth were worrying her bottom lip, but still she

did not look away from him. "What are you going to do?"

"I am going to do what I have been thinking of doing ever since I first caught sight of you. I am going to kiss you."

Her face tinged with pink and he felt her shudder under his hands. "And if I do not want to be kissed?"

"Caroline, Caroline," he said gravely, shaking his head from side to side in reproof. "Surely you are not thinking of telling me another lie. That would be two lies in . . ." He drew his fob watch out of his pocket and consulted it with a grave air. ". . . in just as many minutes. I think it would be better were you to tell me what was really going through your mind at this moment. I think you should tell me the truth."

The truth? Caroline gave a bitter laugh. If she were to tell him exactly what had been going through her mind before he accosted her, he would draw back from her in horror. She was a murderess, if not yet in deed, then certainly in intention.

Before the night had ended, her brother and sisters would be in Heaven and her body would be lying on the floor with a bullet in her brain.

Mr. Savage might not know it, but if he kissed her tonight, he would be kissing a ghost. In her mind she was already dead.

Even so, she *did* want to be kissed by him. Desperately. All the more desperately because this would be the first and last time she would ever be kissed by a man that she desired.

For she did desire him. There was something about him

that attracted her in a way that she did not understand. His eyes spoke of experiences that were not to be had in London, in the world that she knew. His were the mysterious eyes of a man who had learned about love, life, and death in a world far from her own confined sphere.

The knowledge of her certain death hung at her heart, counseling her to make the most of the short time she had left to her. Why should she worry what society might think of her actions? What did she care for the people in the other room so ready to be judge, jury, and executioner? When she had already resolved upon the mortal sins of murder and suicide, it could hardly matter if she were to add an act of simple fornication to her list of sins.

Just ten minutes ago she had been wildly regretting that she would die a virgin.

Now Mr. Savage had interrupted her and announced his intention of kissing her. What else might he be encouraged to do? The conservatory was secluded away from the rest of the house, and even if she were to be caught with him, what did it matter? Her reputation was nothing to her anymore. It would not feed her brother when he was starving or keep her sisters warm when they were shivering with cold at night. She could well risk the loss of her reputation along with her virtue. Neither of them had done her any good till now.

The wildness in her raged to be allowed to live one last time. Really live. With nothing left to lose, she could be a free spirit and choose her own path.

She looked him straight in the eye, meeting his gaze full on. "I *do* want you to kiss me." The words sounded strange to her ears, but she did not falter. They were so forward, so improper. But they were true. She wanted him to kiss her, and to do so much more.

With a desperation borne of finality she leaned into him and pressed her lips against his. Her course was set. Nothing would sway her from it now.

Dominic felt the pressure of her mouth against his with a surge of self-congratulatory triumph. Ah, he'd known all along she was well worth the pursuing. From the moment he'd first seen her, he'd sensed a reckless passion, a lust for life in her that would not easily be quenched. And now she was kissing him as if she was dying of thirst and he was a drink of cool water.

He liked enthusiasm in a woman. Every woman had breasts to fondle, and legs to wrap around a man's waist, and a cunt to welcome a man's cock home. What set one woman's loving apart from another's was far more than the firmness or the ripeness of her body—it was the joy she both gave and took from their joining.

Opening her mouth under his, she met his tongue with her own, kissing him fiercely, as if she wanted to devour him. He drank in her passion, welcoming her touch and urging her further down the path of desire. The world around him disappeared into the night—there was only Caroline and her touch and the sweetness of her kisses that existed for him.

Soon enough her kiss failed to satisfy the growing urgency in his loins. He wanted—no, he needed—to get closer to her. He moved his hands from her face and caressed her throat with a delicacy that belied the strength of his fingers, then moved to cradle her breasts. They were delectable, like the rest of her. Even through the layers of her clothing he could feel their round pertness, begging for the touch of a man.

He brushed his fingers over the tips of her breasts, and was rewarded by a gasp of pleasure and a redoubling of the intensity of her kiss. So, the sweet Caroline liked having her breasts fondled. He would remember that the next time he found himself alone in a conservatory with her.

With his thumb and forefinger he massaged her nipples to hardness. To his surprise, she thrust her breasts forward into his hands, offering him no resistance at all.

He mentally revised his plan in accosting her here. At first he'd thought only to ensure that she was not upset by the obvious defection of the Captain her lover, to dry her tears, and to steal a kiss if the occasion offered. Finding her so responsive, however, had put another idea entirely into his mind.

He wondered if she was as warm and wet and willing as she appeared to be. His cock hardened almost painfully at the thought. If his luck was in, he'd get more than a kiss and a grope of her breasts in the darkness. If Caroline continued to prove this willing, he'd have her skirts in the air and be giving her a good hard fucking before the night was out.

She responded to his hands on her breasts with caresses of her own, running her soft fingers down his neck and back, pulling him toward her to tighten their embrace.

His cock, trapped as it was in his trousers, thrust into her stomach. Instead of pushing away such clear evidence of his arousal and of his intentions, her hands moved down his back to cup his buttocks. She drew him closer to her, squirming against the hardness of his cock, making her own wishes plain. She could not have been clearer if she had begged him in words of one syllable to fuck her.

Damn it, the wench was as ready to be taken as any man could want.

Now that he was sure of her, perversely, he did not want to hurry. Fucking her would be a pleasure to be savored and enjoyed slowly, not to be guiltily hurried over for fear of being caught.

Caroline, it seemed, did not share his desire to linger. Her hands moved to his trousers and began to fumble with the buttons. God, but he wanted the touch of her hands on his cock, stroking him and loving him until he thrust into her pussy.

Maybe he did not really want to wait after all. Deftly, he assisted her fumbling hands to release the fastenings of his clothing, allowing his erection to spring free.

Not content with merely freeing his cock, she slid his trousers down over his hips to his ankles and ran her hands over his naked ass, squeezing his buttocks. Her hands were cool on his naked flesh but they left a trail of fire wherever they went.

Seeming to know just what he wanted without a word being spoken, she sank down to her knees in front of him, her eyes on a level with his jutting cock. "It's purple," she breathed, touching it reverentially with one finger, her eyes as wide as if she had never seen a naked man before. "And I can feel it pulsing under the skin."

"Stroke me."

She did just as he had ordered, stroking him with gentle hands, exploring him with tentative caresses, as if she had never held a man like this in her hands before.

His hands tangled in her hair and he gently guided her mouth to his bobbing erection.

She looked up at him for a moment, astonished, as the purple head of his cock touched her lips. "Kiss me," he said, his voice thick.

"You want me to kiss you there?" Her voice sounded unsure.

He pushed the tip of his cock into her mouth. "I want you to kiss me and lick me and suck on me. Make me as hard as stone for you."

Despite her initial hesitation, she caught on quickly, first tentatively kissing, then lightly licking, exploring him with her mouth and tongue as she had earlier explored him with her hands.

Encouraged by his groans of pleasure, her explorations

gradually grew bolder as she discovered the secrets to giving him pleasure, cupping his tender sac, stroking the base of his erection and licking him all over, then enveloping him in her mouth, swirling her tongue round the sensitive glans on the underside.

He lifted his shirt to afford a better view of Caroline's ministrations. Watching her stroke him and suck on him was turning him on nearly as much as the feeling of her eager hands and her soft, wet mouth on him.

Christ, no wonder her old husband had recently given up the ghost. The tender ministrations of his wife would be enough to fell any old man with a fit of apoplexy.

His distracted musings were brought to a shuddering halt as Caroline took as much of his cock as she could, sucking on him gently while moving her head back and forth. She was fucking him with her mouth.

Damn it, if she kept that up, he was going to spend too soon, before he had even had a taste of her pussy. He pulled away, forcing himself to forgo the delights of her mouth for the hopes of very soon sinking himself deep into her cunt.

He guided her to the wicker chair behind her and seated her with a gentle pressure on her shoulders. "I want to taste you now, just as you tasted me."

Her face once again exhibited a slight unease, but she allowed him to seat her and spread her legs wide apart.

She was so eager, and yet strangely innocent. The combination was utterly irresistible.

He reached under her skirts, moving his hands up her silk-clad legs until smooth silk stockings made way for cotton bloomers.

The bloomers would have to go. He found the drawstrings that held them closed and tugged on them to loosen them, pulling them free. She provided tacit permission by lifting her hips and allowing her undergarment to slide down her silk stockings. He pulled them over her ankles and tossed them aside.

Now that her pesky bloomers were disposed of, she was open to his gaze. Lifting her skirts, he pushed her legs farther apart. The dim gaslight illuminated her wet cunt. The fine reddish blond hair that adorned her head also provided a gold surround for her pussy. Her lips were parted, revealing the glistening pinkness inside.

He admired the sight for a few moments before moving his head closer and inhaling her heady scent. He loved pussies. He loved looking, smelling, touching, tasting them. They represented the center of a woman, the essence of what made women special.

Finally he allowed himself a taste, his tongue lightly flicking in and out of her opening.

At the touch of his tongue on her pussy she gave a start and squeaked with surprise. Her body tensed under him.

Ah, so old Mr. Clemens had not been a fan of licking his wife's pussy. More fool him. And he had no doubt that the Captain had been too selfish a lover to take pleasure in the sweet taste of his Caroline. Their loss was most definitely his gain.

Feeling unaccountably satisfied that he was introducing her to a new game, he continued to lick her and suck at her, hoping he had not lost his touch at pleasuring a woman in this way.

Her hands were now tangled in his hair, grasping him hard, but pulling him toward her rather than pushing him away.

Encouraged by her whimpers of pleasure, he moved his lapping tongue to the center of her pleasure. Parting her cunt with his hands, he ran the flat of his tongue over and over her clit, causing her back to arch in delight.

Her gasps of pleasure grew louder and she wriggled down in the chair so her ass rested on the edge, then leaned back and held her legs open wider than before. Spread-eagled as she was before him, she offered him access to every intimate part of her body.

He took advantage of the position to move his tongue to her ass, where he tasted her sweet tight hole, his nose buried in her cunt.

His own cock was throbbing painfully. Knowing how close he was to having her completely was tormenting him, but still he continued to lick her.

He wanted to taste her orgasm before he thrust his cock into her pussy. He wanted her to come apart for him under his mouth and fingers, making her pussy drip with juice, making her soft and open for him.

With long lingering strokes of his tongue, he lapped at her, over and over. Her body tensed with desire, wound tighter and tighter with every stroke. Holding her buttocks firmly, he increased the pressure as Caroline's breath started to come in short pants. Suddenly her entire body stiffened, the blood pulsed through her pussy in waves, and she cried out as she came.

She flopped back in the chair, panting, her face pink from her exertions. "I never knew it could be like that." Her eyes were full of wonderment and, surprisingly, of gratitude.

His own desire throbbed urgently now, desperate to be sated.

With Caroline still seated on the chair, he afforded her no respite as he rubbed his stone-hard cock up and down her swollen cunt, making it slick with her juices. She was ready for him, and he was more than ready for her. He had been aching for her for what seemed like hours now.

Slowly he pushed into her. Though her pussy was dripping with juice, it was a tight squeeze for him.

He paused halfway, thinking he felt a slight resistance, but before he could think too much of it she pulled him close, causing him to be completely engulfed.

The deed was done. She had a man's part thrust up to the hilt in her body, and she had felt it breaching her maidenhood. She was no longer a virgin.

Ah, but she was glad that she had had the courage to experience loving before she died. What a waste it would have been to go to her death without having experienced the mind-numbing pleasure that she had felt with his mouth and tongue on her most private parts. She had had to bite her tongue to keep herself from screaming out when that first rush of intense pleasure swept over her.

And now the feeling of him inside her was kindling her desire anew.

She thrust herself against him, pushing him deeper inside her. Never had she felt so alive as she did in this moment, with the taste of him on her tongue and his manly part buried deep inside her. She wanted the moment to last forever.

Oh, how she wanted to live.

With his cock buried, Dominic kissed her deeply. He then started a rhythmic motion, loving her with his whole body. Slowly and deeply he thrust into her, the pleasure building with every stroke. Her body welcomed him, her pussy muscles closing around him so tightly it was as if she wanted to keep him inside her forever.

Over and over he thrust into her until he saw the signs of her orgasm approach once more. Without warning, he withdrew completely. "Turn over. I want to take you from behind as animals fuck each other. Nothing but pleasure."

In a daze of lust, she allowed him to flip her over. He placed her knees on the chair seat, tipping her ass up into the air, with the backrest for her to grip.

As soon as she was firmly anchored, he parted her firm, white buttocks and without hesitation plunged back into her open cunt.

God, she felt even better in this position than she had in the last one. He wanted to fuck her a thousand ways to Christmas, until they had exhausted every possible way they could fuck each other.

With little short strokes he brought himself close to orgasm before relieving the approach of the inevitable with deeper, longer strokes that caused her to cry out in pleasure.

He paused a moment with his cock nearly completely removed, to admire the sight of it slick with her juices at the entrance to her pussy. Before he'd had enough of admiring the sight, she pushed her ass back, once again burying him in her soft wetness.

Reaching in front of her, he teased her sensitive clit, while he made short movements deep inside her.

Each time he reached the deepest part of her, a whimper of pleasure escaped her and her entire body shuddered. "Please," she moaned, writhing against his hand and begging him to release her from her sensual torment. "Please."

With that he could hold off no longer. Releasing her clit, he grabbed her buttocks tightly and rode her with full fast strokes until he felt his seed about to spurt.

With a cry of his own he buried himself as far as he could, his whole body shuddering with release as stream after stream of hot liquid jetted from him.

As the hotness of his seed spurted inside her, he felt waves of pleasure wash through her body. Her pussy muscles clenched in orgasm, extending his own pleasure and milking him of every last drop of seed.

As her orgasm washed over her and then slowly receded, she collapsed bonelessly onto the chair. Dominic fell on top of her, still inside her, his cock slowly losing its hardness in utter satiation.

He moved to one side, allowing Caroline some room to breathe. "You are truly a surprising woman," he murmured, brushing a tendril of hair away from her eyes. "So proper in public, so wild in private. You intrigue me."

Now that her passion was spent, he could see reality intrude into her mind once more. There was a sadness in her that his lovemaking had not dissipated, though the brittleness was no longer so evident.

"I shall visit you. Soon." He was already looking forward to having her again, this time on a bed where he could undress her fully and feast on the sight of her nakedness without fear of interruption.

Now that he had tasted her, he knew that once would not be enough for him. Already his cock was stirring beside her, nudging against her hip, wanting another taste of her perfection.

She looked gravely into his eyes, and he got the uncomfortable feeling he was not looking into the same eyes as before. "I do not think we will ever meet again, Mr. Savage," she said with a slight smile. "But I thank you, from the bottom of my heart, for what you have shown me here tonight."

And with that she raised herself off the chair, smoothed down her skirts, and without a backward glance or even a thought for her bloomers lying discarded in the corner, walked out of the door.

Three

Dominic watched her walk away from him, her hips sway-ing. Caroline Clemens was full of surprises. So hot and eager, yet so inexperienced in the art of lovemaking. The combination had been a heady turn on, even for him, who prided himself on his coolness and on being impervious to all feminine wiles. If his time in India had taught him noth-ing else, he had learned how to harness the power of human sensuality, to use it as a tool or as a weapon, but always to keep it under his control and never let it overpower his good sense.

These few stolen moments with Caroline had come close to destroying the teachings he lived by. She had affected him more powerfully than any woman had before, which made her both infinitely more alluring and infinitely more danger-ous than other women. His inexplicably strong attraction to her must be kept tamed so it did not grow so powerful that it broke free of all restraint and devoured everything in its path.

Even though he was sated for now, he surprised himself by not wanting to let her go. She belonged to him, body and soul. His lovemaking had cast all thought of the Captain out of her mind, he was sure of it.

Yet if so—and he was sure it *was* so—why was she walking away from him so steadily, not so much as turning her head to gaze after him? Her coolness infuriated him. He wanted to be the cool one, the sensible one, while she burned with a passion for him that she could neither resist nor deny.

Once the door closed behind her, he clambered back into his trousers, smoothed down his clothing and prepared to join the company again. His dalliance with the delectable Caroline notwithstanding, he still had some important matters of business to attend to tonight. Distractions were all very well in their place, but they must not be allowed to interfere with the real business of the day—making money.

The room was all abuzz with quiet chatter when he rejoined his cronies. Something momentous had clearly happened while he had been otherwise engaged in the conservatory, as practically every woman in the room had gathered together in a tight huddle. The whole lot of them were whispering animatedly at each other, sounding just like sparrows in a tree at sunset.

He turned to Adam Farrell, a banker who had befriended him when he first returned from India. "What are all the women fussing about?"

Adam shrugged. "Something about the Clemens girl, I believe."

"The Clemens girl?" Not the Clemens widow? It was an odd way of referring to her, but he supposed she was hardly more than a girl.

"The good-looking blonde in the black dress," Adam explained. "You must be acquainted with her. I saw you talking to her earlier this evening. You seemed particularly engrossed in the conversation."

He shrugged off Adam's comment. His preoccupation with the delicious Caroline was his own affair. "What about her?"

"Her father, Isaac Clemens, was a speculator, and not a very good one. He lost everything and then shot himself."

"Isaac Clemens was her father? Not her husband?" Damn it, had he been so blinded by lust that his good sense had utterly deserted him? "She was in full mourning. I thought by her dress that she must be his widow."

"Clemens was a widower, his wife died some years ago. When he died, the Clemens girl lost the dowry he had promised."

"She was in widow's weeds," he murmured, more to himself than to Adam. "In full black." Oh Christ, what had he done? He'd assumed she was a sexually frustrated—or an unfaithful—young widow more relieved than upset at the death of her elderly husband. It had never crossed his mind that she could possibly be anything else.

So much for acting the sophisticated lover. He'd tossed her black skirts above her waist and fucked her hard and fast from behind. Quite likely she'd been a virgin before tonight, too, for all that she'd been as randy as a two-bit piece and had welcomed his fucking like one born to the game. No wonder she had seemed so inexperienced. But he'd been so cunt-struck that not even her obvious newness to the game had been enough to stop him.

"She was due to be married in a week or two, but her fiancé, it seems, has just tossed her over for a wealthier prospect."

"She was to be married?"

"To Captain Bellamy." Adam made a face. "Not that I ever thought much of him, but a husband is a husband, especially when you have nothing but your pretty face to recommend you."

His assessment of Captain Bellamy's motives had been accurate, then. The Captain's loss had been his gain, and the delectable Miss Clemens had been ripe for the taking. "What will happen to the girl now?" He hoped she had no other man waiting in the wings wanting to marry her—at least not until he'd had his fill of her. Already his cock was half standing in his trousers at the thought of fucking her again.

"Girls. There are a half-dozen Clemens sisters at least.

The one here tonight is the eldest. They have no other family that I know of—leastways my wife knows of none, and she is usually *au fait* with all the gossip. Old Isaac will have left something for them to live on, I suppose. An annuity or some such that could not be touched by his creditors. It's what any decent man in his situation would do before he pulled the trigger."

With no father and no husband and little money to call her own, poor Caroline would be desperately vulnerable. If she had half an ounce of sense, she would be looking around for a convenient man who would help her support herself—for the right consideration, of course.

A man just like him. Not inconveniently committed elsewhere, and willing to be generous to a woman who captured his fancy.

Dominic smiled to himself. That would explain why she had given him such an unexpected welcome in the conservatory. She had sensed his obvious interest in her and thought to snare him while she had the chance.

His smile widened. There was no doubt about it—she was a clever woman, and with a solid practical streak to her as well. Though some of her narrow-minded set would frown upon her actions, he admired them. He appreciated her courage and good sense almost as much as he craved her soft, white body.

Dammit, but he would gladly sign up to pay her bills if it meant he could keep her in his bed for a good while longer.

Though he would lay good money on it that she had been an innocent until tonight, she was hot and eager enough to keep him interested for months.

Caroline walked through the dark streets alone, arriving home just after midnight. Her interlude with Mr. Savage had not caused her to change her decision even by the slightest degree. On the contrary, it had only made her more determined on her course of action. She had cut off her last possible hope of rescue. No longer did she have even her virginity, for what it was worth, to bargain with.

Not that she had been able to bargain with it when Captain Bellamy gave her the opportunity earlier in the evening. The thought of becoming his mistress, when she should have been his wife, disgusted her.

And who else would want her anyway? Now that she was no longer a virgin, her worth in the marketplace where human flesh was traded would be even less than the paltry two hundred a year the Captain had offered her.

Her face hardened. She would never forgive him for driving her to these straits. If she had her way, her very ghost would come back and haunt him when she was dead, and drive him to madness and despair. It would be no more than he deserved.

Her evening slippers in her hand, she unlocked the front door and crept through the silent house to her papa's study, alert for the tiniest creak or rustle that might disturb her sisters and brother. They could not wake. Not now.

The pistol, she knew, was back in the gun cabinet, locked away where her young brother could not accidentally get to it.

But the key? She thought hard for a moment in the stillness of the night.

Then she remembered. After Papa's accident, she had put the key away in the top drawer of his desk, where he always kept it.

She rummaged around for it among the mess of papers. Poor Papa had never been good at keeping his papers in order. That had been his downfall in the end.

Her fingers came across something cold and hard. Ah, there it was.

She was shaking so much she could hardly pick it up, and then it took her an age to fit it into the lock and turn it. Finally the cabinet door swung open. There was the pistol that had murdered her papa, the same pistol that would soon claim the lives of the rest of her family.

It was heavy, heavier than she had expected. Holding it carefully by the butt, she pulled open the hammer and rotated the cylinder, counting the bullets one by one as she did so. Six brass cartridges gleamed in the dim light.

One cartridge had been fired. The bullet that had killed her father. Only five were left. Five was one too few.

She steeled her soul against the despair that welled up in

her. No matter that she would not have the quick death she had hoped for of a bullet in the brain. Her bed was made with good, strong linen sheets to make a rope out of to hang herself when the rest was done.

She thumbed the hammer shut again. There, she was ready. She had to hurry and not falter along the way. Though the first shot would wake them all, she still hoped to finish her grisly task before they fully realized what was afoot.

The pistol held firmly in both hands, she opened the door to the study and held still for a moment, listening. No one stirred. The entire household, such as it was, was fast asleep.

Her stomach clenched in pain as she began to creep toward the stairs that led up to the bedrooms on the upper floor. Her brother had to be the first. He was the youngest, and of all of them he would understand the least why she had to do this.

He was asleep, his small body curled up under the bedclothes and a half smile on his face, as if he were in the midst of pleasant dreams.

She knelt down beside him and kissed his sleeping face. "Please, darling, forgive me," she whispered as she brought the pistol to his temple. Silent tears were streaming down her face. "This is for the best, I swear it."

She brought the hammer back, cocking it, the pistol making a loud click in the silence of the night.

He stirred under the bedclothes and his eyes opened. He

did not seem frightened to see his sister in front of him, holding a gun to his head. "Are you going to shoot me?" he whispered. "Like Papa shot himself?"

She did not answer. She could not. Her tongue was stuck to the roof of her mouth with the horror of what she must do. Her finger moved on the trigger, pulling it back a little ways.

He sensed her hesitance and put out a small hand to comfort her. "I do not mind. I will be brave and not cry out," he promised her.

As she pulled the trigger, the strength in her arm faltered and the muzzle of the gun dropped away to the floor. The pistol disturbed the silence with a loud report, blowing a jagged hole in the floorboards at her feet.

She sank down bonelessly onto the bed, staring at the hole in the floor with horror. "Forgive me, Teddy, but I cannot do it. I cannot shoot you."

He sat up in the bed and threw his arms around her neck. "Do not cry, Caroline. I am glad you did not shoot me. Who would look after you all now that Papa is gone if I am dead, too?"

The noise had wakened the other girls. One by one they came running into Teddy's bedroom, their eyes wide with fright.

"What is it, Caroline? What has happened?"

There were no words to explain what she had just tried to do. No words to explain away the horror of her lack of courage, the disaster of failure.

Teddy spoke up, his boyish treble firm. "It was an accident. Caroline was showing me how to load Papa's gun and it went off by accident."

Emily looked suspiciously at him. "Caroline was showing you how to load Papa's gun? In the middle of the night?" She turned her gaze to her sister. "Caroline?"

Caroline could not answer. She could not even look at her sister. Uncontrollable sobs wracked her body. Clutched in her fingers, the pistol burned her to the bottom of her soul. She had nearly killed Teddy, her own brother, the darling baby of them all. How could she live with herself after tonight? How could she live with her failure?

"I begged her to. I couldn't sleep," Teddy lied resolutely.

Emily's sharp gaze went around the room. Although she clearly did not like what she saw, she put her arms around her younger sisters and drew them into a huddle where they could not see the damage the shot had caused. "Next time you can't sleep, ask for a glass of warm milk instead," she suggested wryly. "It makes less noise."

"Nobody was hurt," Teddy reassured her. "You can all go back to bed."

With one last suspicious glance at the pair of them, Emily shepherded the other three girls out of the room.

As soon as the door shut behind them, Teddy put an arm around Caroline's shoulders. "They are gone now. You can stop crying."

The kind gesture only redoubled her tears. "You lied for me."

His face went white in the moonlight. "Are you angry that I told a lie?" She could see his mind whirring over in the dim light. "Are you angry with me? Is that why you were going to shoot me?"

She reached out and ruffled his hair. How precious he was to her. How precious all her siblings were. They were all she had to cling to, all that she had left. "I am not angry with you. I am just ... sad." What would a young boy know of the utter hopelessness of their situation, of the despair that gripped her soul whenever she thought of what must befall them all? She had tried to save him from such knowledge, but she could not.

"You are sad because Papa is dead and we have no money."

"I am sad because Papa is dead," she agreed. "And you are right that we have no money. None at all."

"Do we have enough money to buy a pony?" Having a pony of his own had been his dearest wish for months.

"No, not enough money for a pony." Poor Teddy. He would never get the pony their papa had promised him. "We do not even have enough money to buy food for tomorrow's dinner." She hated having to burden him with the details of their situation, but he had a right to know. She had given him that right tonight.

He squared his shoulders. "I am the man of the house now. I will earn the money for all our dinners."

He was so brave she wanted to cry all over again. "How will you earn our dinners?"

"I can sell matches on the street. I have seen other boys do that."

"It would not be enough," she said, hating to burst his bubble. "It would not be enough even if we all sold matches on the streets."

He was silent for a moment, deep in thought. "Will we starve to death, then?"

She shook her head. "No, Teddy, we will not starve. When our money runs out and we have to sell the house, we will go to the workhouse. The kind people there will take us in and feed us."

Dominic cursed under his breath at the ill-timed crisis with one of his major investments that had called him away from London at this juncture. Though ordinarily he would have been pleased to escape the dull, gray monotony of London skies for the clean air of one of the smaller country towns through which his railways ran, right at this moment London held a major attraction for him.

The last place he wanted to be was in this godforsaken inn in this tiny town where the beds were bad, the food was worse, and the inhabitants demanding in the extreme. If it weren't for their unreasonable demands and the stringent conditions they wanted to place on him before he could build his railway through their land—the railway that would put their town on the map and bring them unlooked for prosperity—he would still be in London. Curled up not in a cold, lumpy, single bed by himself, but in his own clean and sweet-smelling bed, pillowed next to the delightfully soft and warm Miss Caroline.

Caroline Clemens. He rolled the name around on his tongue. It tasted sweet, as sweet as she had tasted that night in the conservatory of the oh so very proper Finsburys. A grin crept over his face as he thought of the forbiddingly fierce and purple-turbaned matron whose conservatory he had christened in such a manner. Thank Heaven that Mrs. Amelia Finsbury had no idea as to what transpired between him and the delectable Caroline among the potted ferns, or she would never speak to him again or invite him to another of her soirees.

Offending Mrs. Finsbury would, certainly, have had certain advantages. If he could thoroughly upset her, she would no longer try quite so hard to throw one of her dour-faced daughters at him. Her machinations so far to get him to take an interest in one of them had been embarrassingly, and at times painfully, obvious.

When he had expressed his surprise at the transparency of her efforts to get his attention, his fellows merely laughed at his naiveté. Such tactics were quite the norm in London. Every father wanted to get his daughters suitably settled in the world, to sons-in-law who would not embarrass the family with spendthrift habits or indigent relatives.

Social niceties were quite different from what they had been in India, where he was born and where, with the exception of a few miserable years at boarding school in the north of England, he had lived all his life. Until now.

Society in India had tried hard, too hard, to mimic exactly the manners and customs of the mother country. But nothing, not even English manners, could survive in another country, another culture, completely unscathed.

Despite his great wealth, he was forced to tread carefully in order to avoid giving offense to the grand society matrons such as Amelia Finsbury who had accepted him into their houses and their society. Fucking Caroline Clemens in the conservatory at a soiree was without a doubt enough of a social solecism to get him barred forever from the houses of respectable folk.

Not that he cared for anyone's feelings in the matter. Other than Caroline's, of course. He would not like to see her reputation shredded. She was his woman now, his glorious English lover. With their first kiss, he had claimed her. She belonged to him.

His groin tightened at the mere thought of her. She was far from the upright icicle maiden that he'd been warned to expect before he left India. English girls, he was informed by more than one well-meaning friend, were unfortunately not like Indian girls, not like the wonderful woman he had married. Maya, his dear, beloved Maya, whose loss had left a wound in his soul that not even time could heal.

Girls in India had their blood heated by the hot, hot sun. They were openly passionate, and none of them that he'd ever taken to his bed had any qualms about enjoying the act of love just as much as he had. Maya had certainly enticed him with her lush body, giving in to him one minute and the next minute drawing away, until she had him wrapped up in knots so tight that he had not been able to escape her.

Truth to tell, he had never wanted to escape her. If she had not died, he would be with her still, as faithful as he had been since he first met her and fell in love with her, harder and faster than he would have believed. With one sideways look from her dark eyes, she had set his head to spinning. Only her death could have chased him halfway around the world, away from the land he loved and back to cold, gray England.

Girls in England, he had been warned, were not like Maya. They were as cold and passionless as the cold, gray English skies. Water, not blood, ran through their veins. The only thing that could put a fire in their eyes and in their bellies was the prospect of marrying a man with money, lots of money. Everything else left them unmoved. They submitted to a man's embrace only for the sake of capturing a wealthy husband.

The avid-eyed matrons he had met, eligible daughters in tow, only confirmed those warnings. The gleam of greed that he saw sparkle in the eyes of every seemingly demure young virgin he met had given him a decided distaste for English girls.

Until he met Caroline. In her, he had found the exception that proved the rule. She had not asked a single delicate yet probing question as to the state of his finances or the credit-worthiness of his investments. His prospects, the ready cash held for him in the bank of England, were of no interest to her.

No, from the expression in her eyes, she had only ever been interested in him, Dominic the man. She did not care about Dominic the newly arrived from India tycoon with business interests in half the railways in England. Chances were she did not even know. Emboldened by the smoldering desire he espied in her, he'd had the temerity to introduce himself, after all, rather than making use of a go-between. No friendly acquaintance had pointed him out to her as a good catch, encouraging her to wangle an introduction, an invitation to dance, and a chance to flutter her eyelashes at him.

He would wager that Caroline Clemens never fluttered her eyelashes. She had too much pride in her self-worth to make use of such a transparent and silly ploy. Honesty and directness was more her style.

She had captivated him with the plain expression of her wants and desires, especially seeing as he had figured largely in those wants of hers. Enticement, not submission, was her game.

Although he had certainly wanted her, he was not the only culpable party. Not content with being a passive recipient of his attentions, she had urged him on, moaning and clutching at him and leaving him in no doubt as to what she needed. His tongue was in her mouth and his cock was sunk deep into her pussy before he'd had time to think better of his impetuous actions.

She had welcomed his fucking, maybe hoping that he would be in a position to help ease her financial troubles, but first and foremost because she had desired him.

He turned his pillow over, trying in vain to ignore the insistent throbbing in his groin that assaulted him whenever he thought of Caroline. The damned pillow refused to mold comfortably to his head. It was so hard and lumpy the damned innkeeper must have filled it with gravel. The lack of such a basic creature comfort as a decent down pillow did not improve his temper any.

He reached down and stroked his cock, hardened by thoughts of Caroline. Damn it, if he couldn't have her in his bed right now, he could think of her while he pleasured himself.

He could remember the taste of her pussy and the tightness of her cunt as he thrust his cock into it. He could imagine the sounds she would make as he undressed her until she was naked for him. Laying her on the bed, he would part her nether lips and thrust first one finger and then another inside her, fucking her gently with his hands. Only when she was dripping wet and begging for him to come on top of her would he climb between her legs and pump his cock into her.

And then, when she was well fucked and about to come, he would turn her over and, his cock slick with her cunt juice, thrust it into her sweet ass. Her tight hole would grip him like a glove. She would explode under him, crying and writhing out in ecstasy and begging him for more.

He stopped stroking his cock. There really was no need for him to spend a lonely night with only his warm hand for company. He was after all a free man, with needs like any other, and the innkeeper was bound to know of a local woman who could satisfy him. No doubt a good part of his trade came from arranging to service similar requests from travelers.

Leaping out of the lumpy bed, he stood naked in the cool air and looked down at his still hard cock. "Just a few moments, my friend, and you'll be warm and well-housed. Be patient."

With that he threw on his clothes and went downstairs to visit briefly with the innkeeper.

Barely fifteen minutes later there was a knock at his door. Opening it revealed a pretty young woman with a tired look about her eyes, as if life had already started to overwhelm her.

She first examined him, and then peered into the room appraising him and the state of his luggage. No doubt she met all sorts in her business. "You want some company this evening?"

Evidently deciding all was in order, without further invitation she walked into his room. "I'm Rosie," she said, holding out her hand. "Two shillings for half an hour."

Wordlessly, he handed over the two shillings she asked for.

She grabbed them and tucked them away in her pocket as quick as winking. "What do you fancy, then?" she asked, more cheerfully now.

He was already halfway regretting his decision to buy a whore. "The usual, I suppose."

With a few deft moves she unfastened her buttons and let her gown fall to the floor. She wore nothing underneath.

While no Caroline, she was fine enough. Not too skinny, but pleasingly plump with smallish breasts and a fine patch of blond hair at the top of her legs.

"Now you, then. Let's be having you." Without ceremony she squatted and released his trousers, which fell to his ankles, revealing his semirigid cock.

"Ooh, that's lovely," she said perfunctorily, as if remarking on the weather. "Such a nice cock."

Still, she wrapped her lips around the head without hesitation and began to pump the base with her hand. As she continued her ministrations he removed his jacket and shirt, making him as naked as she.

As soon as his cock was fully hard, she led him to the bed and lay down, legs splayed, pulling her pussy lips apart to reveal the wetness inside. "Come on then, sir, give me that cock."

Gazing at her open cunt, he suddenly wondered if any passing travelers had given her a dose. The possibility made him lose whatever enthusiasm he had left for her pussy.

In any case, it was really Caroline he wanted. What a fool he had been to think a two shilling whore would be any replacement for her.

Still, he'd paid the woman now. She might as well provide

him with the release he needed. He shook his head at her offer. "Keep going with your mouth."

She eyed him shrewdly from the bed. "That would be an extra shilling, if that's what you're wanting."

It was worth it to avoid a dose of the clap. "You'll have your extra shilling," he promised. A dose was one thing he did *not* want to pass on to Caroline.

Sitting up and grabbing his buttocks, she once more engulfed his cock in her mouth.

He closed his eyes and imagined it was Caroline sitting before him, sucking his cock in that enthusiastic way of hers. He imagined softly caressing her breasts, teasing the nipples to hard points. In his mind's eye he saw her lying on the bed, alabaster white in the gaslight. He could still taste her gorgeous pussy, wet and musky, and so soft.

Rosie continued lightly sucking on the head of his cock, pumping at the base to make him come faster. With her other hand she massaged his balls, expertly pulling on the sac while grazing a finger over his sensitive asshole. As he felt his orgasm approach, he could almost feel his cock plunging into Caroline's hot cunt over and over till she cried out in pleasure.

At that last, delicious thought, his seed splattered over Rosie's lips and chin as she pulled her head away at the last moment. Holding her head, he had her give his cock a few more licks, his heart rate returning slowly to normal as reality intruded once more.

With a sigh of disappointment he stepped back from her. If only Caroline had been here, he was certain he would not even have noticed the discomfort of the bed. And their lovemaking would just be starting, not finishing.

Rosie stood and wiped at her face with his shirt. As she pulled on her dress, she reminded him of his debt. "So, the extra shilling, then?"

Giving the girl her dues, he escorted her wordlessly to the door, his thoughts back on Caroline once more. Damn it, why was he even bothering to argue the point with the residents of nowhere? He could afford to meet their demands. Tomorrow morning he would play the generous benefactor, give them what they had asked for and more, and escape back to London and to Caroline.

Caroline stood motionless in the drawing room, watching out the window as the bailiffs trudged up to the front door in the early morning light. She had put off the evil day as long as she could, but there was no avoiding it now. Today their house was forfeit and all the contents were to be sold. By noon she and her brother and sisters would be homeless. By dinnertime they would all be homeless and hungry.

Each moment she stood in her drawing room surrounded by her family was stolen from the jaws of Time.

She could hear the bailiffs in the hallway. One of them strode in through the drawing room door. He stopped short at the sight of the six of them clustered together in the window.

"The auction starts at nine o'clock sharp," he said brusquely. "You'd better be off before then."

She gathered her black shawl more closely around her shoulders. It was time to leave the place she had called home for all her life. Now even if Dominic Savage wished to find her again as he had promised, he would not know where to look for her. "Emily, Louisa, Beatrice, Dorothea, Teddy," she said, counting them all off to make sure they were all there. "Come, it is time to go."

It was a long, dismal walk from Bloomsbury Square to the workhouse in St. Giles, but they had not even enough pennies to take the omnibus part of the way. They were no better than beggars now.

Before they had gone a mile, Caroline's legs were aching. After another mile her feet were rubbed red and raw by the hard leather of her walking boots, her sturdiest pair of shoes and the ones she had elected to take with her to the workhouse. Her kid slippers would be of no use to her there.

Her sisters were no better off. Louisa was already limping badly, though she did not breathe a word of complaint. Teddy was struggling along manfully, but he was clearly the most exhausted of them all.

A patch of common land covered in grass and trees beckoned to her. She sat down under a tree to take off her boots, and the others sank down wearily next to her.

Emily fidgeted uncomfortably while the others rested.

"Shouldn't we keep going? We will never make it to the work-house by dark if we do not hurry."

Caroline stroked Teddy's hair. Almost as soon as they stopped he had fallen asleep with his head in her lap, and was snoring softly. "Are you in such a hurry to get to the work-house?"

Emily flushed. "We must sleep somewhere tonight."

"We cannot go on just yet. We will wait until Teddy wakes."

"And if he sleeps too long?"

Caroline smoothed away a lock of hair that had fallen over his eyes. "Poor child. Let him sleep while he may. It would be better if he were never to wake."

Emily shot a sidelong glance at their three younger sisters, who were happily engaged in making daisy chains a few feet away. She leaned in toward Caroline until their heads were almost touching. "The gun?" she whispered.

Caroline bowed her head. "It would have been easier for all of us," she whispered, "but I did not have the courage."

"Teddy knew?"

"And lied about it to protect me."

Emily's eyes softened. "That is a heavy burden for a young boy to carry. No wonder he is worn-out. I would not wake him for the world."

"You are right, though. We will never reach the workhouse tonight."

"The weather is still warm." Emily patted the grass beside

her as happily as if it were a soft feather bed. "We can sleep outside on the commons for a night. If we all huddle close together we will keep warm enough."

Caroline could still feel the weight of her papa's gun in her hands. If only she had kept it, hidden it somehow from the creditors and their bailiffs, she would still have the option of setting them all free. But it was too late now. Her courage had deserted her at a crucial juncture, and it was too late for them even if she could muster enough bravery in her soul. By now Papa's gun would be sold at auction to the highest bidder, and with it had gone any hope of an easy exit from the world. "I should have shot us all while I had the chance."

"Do not think such evil thoughts, Caroline. While we are alive, there is hope." Emily gave a small smile and took Caroline's hand in hers. "The human spirit is a funny thing. Even now, even though I must sleep in a ditch tonight, cold and wet and hungry, I would not choose to die." Her eyes were brimming with tears. "I want to live, Caroline. It is selfish of me, I know, but even though I must go to the workhouse and labor for my bread, I want so much to live."

Caroline squeezed Emily's hand in hers. She had no words to tell her sister how much she shared the sentiment. Even now she wanted to live so much that her desire frightened her. She wanted to live and to see Dominic again, to have him look at her with his eyes filled with desire, as he had looked at her that night in the conservatory. "Thank you, Emily. Thank you for sharing the burden with me."

She sat on the grass, watching her family with a measure of peace creeping over her soul. Though their father had forsaken them, and the Captain had deserted her, and even Dominic Savage had loved her and left her without a second thought, still she would carry on. Emily had lent her strength to go on when she had none left to draw on. With Emily by her side, the two of them would outface the world and keep their family together.

Emily was right. While there was life, there was still hope. A faint and weak hope it might be, but it was still there to light up the darkness of her world.

Her newfound determination lasted her through the whole of the long, exhausting day of endless walking. Despite their best efforts, by the time night fell they had walked little more than half the distance they needed to go.

Caroline was exhausted from her efforts to keep up the spirits of the younger ones, encouraging and cajoling them to keep on walking when they faltered, entertaining them with stories of when they were little, and holding out the promise of hot food and a warm bed to lie in when they finally reached their destination.

As they were crossing a patch of common land, it was Louisa who finally called a halt to their journey by dropping to the ground in a dead faint. Beatrice gave a cry of alarm and sank down on her knees next to her, cradling Louisa's head in her lap.

It was only a moment before Louisa sat up again, her face a picture of bewilderment, but Caroline died a thousand deaths in that moment. Her sisters were young, and Louisa had never been very strong. In her haste to reach shelter she had pushed them too hard.

Louisa pushed her hair back from her face. "I am sorry," she murmured as she tried to struggle to her feet again. "I did not mean to."

"You have nothing to be sorry for," Beatrice said, almost fiercely. "You could not help it, could she, Caroline?"

"Indeed she could not. It is my fault that I made you keep on walking when I knew you were weary. Do not get up. We will rest now."

"Right here?" Louisa queried.

Beatrice looked around her doubtfully but bit her lip and said nothing.

Dorothea and Teddy simply plumped down on the grass with sighs of relief and began to unlace their boots. Dorothea was singing happily under her breath, as if she did not have a care in the world.

"Leave your boots on," Emily counseled them, joining them on the grass. "They will help to keep your feet warm."

Caroline shared around the last of their provisions. It was a meager supper they made, with only a hunk of bread, a scrap of cheese, and a withered apple to sustain them after all their walking. Teddy and Dorothea wolfed theirs in no time and looked hopefully at Caroline for more, but she shook her head.

"We have nothing more until tomorrow." It was one of the reasons she had pushed them so hard today. The walk tomorrow, on empty bellies and feet that were already sore, would be far harder even than today's.

In the disappointed silence that followed, Louisa tried to slip Teddy her apple, but Beatrice stopped her with a growl. "You need the food yourself. He can have mine if he's still hungry."

Caroline silenced them both with a look. "I have shared the food evenly." It was only a small lie. She was not hungry so it was no hardship for her to do with less than the others. "You must each eat what you have been given. We all need to keep up our strength. None of us will manage if one of us falls behind."

Louisa bent her head, flushing at the mild rebuke, and obediently ate her apple.

Their supper finished, they stumbled over the grass to a massive oak tree that grew by the side of the lane. Its widespreading branches would afford them a little shelter from the morning dew.

The six of them lay down in a small hollow at the base of the tree, the younger ones in the middle where they would be better protected from the chill night breezes. She and Emily lay down at each end and spread their shawls over them all.

As Caroline dropped off to sleep, the last thought that went through her mind was a heartfelt prayer for no rain.

★ ★ ★

The morning dawned gray and misty. The air was dank and clingy with wet, and though there was only a light drizzle, it seemed to penetrate through Caroline's clothes and skin, down to her very bones.

She woke before it was light, having slept only fitfully. The cold of the ground had seeped into her, leaving her chilled and miserable. Carefully she disengaged herself from the pile of sleeping bodies, stood up and stretched her aching limbs. This morning she hurt in places that she had never known even existed before.

One by one her sisters stirred sleepily and got to their feet, none of them tempted to linger on the ground. They made a sorry picture with red-rimmed eyes that stood out starkly in their pales faces, and hair that looked like birds had been nesting in it all night. She put a hand to her own hair, making a halfhearted attempt to smooth it, even knowing how futile the attempt would be.

What would Mr. Savage think if he saw her now? The thought made her smile wryly. No doubt his sensibilities would be shocked that she had slept out under the stars all night and was preparing to break her fast on any blackberries she could gather from the hedgerows. He would not think her beautiful any longer, if indeed he ever had. His words of flattery had no doubt been just that—fine words well calculated to get her exactly where he wanted her.

It was her shame that he had succeeded, her shame that she

had allowed him to take her virginity with so little ceremony. She had not even tried to resist him, or put up a fight. On the contrary, she had welcomed his attentions, and allowed him to do shocking things to her body. Even worse, she had practiced similarly on his body, exploring it and touching it and tasting it without a thought for all the precepts she had been brought up with.

Resolutely she turned her back on her shame, forcing it to the dark recesses of her mind. Her virginity, or her lack of it, ought to be her last worry right now. She had more practical concerns to worry about, such as how she was to keep them all strong enough to make it to the workhouse before another night fell. Though they were trying manfully to hide it, all her sisters looked as exhausted and as dispirited as she felt. All of them, that is, except for Dorothea, whose natural good spirits shone through even in such moments as these.

Oblivious to the discomfort, Teddy was the last to wake. Eventually he, too, rolled over and opened his eyes to the new day. "What's for breakfast?" he demanded before he had even gotten to his feet.

"Blackberries. And the sooner you get up and going, the sooner you'll have them in your belly."

That had him on his feet right away. "Blackberries. Goody, goody. Where are they?"

"Growing on the bushes. You'll have to find them before you can eat them."

"I bet I find the most," he said as he ran on ahead of the

group, with Dorothea hard on his heels. "I'm the best black-berry finder of all of us."

"No you're not. I am," Dorothea chanted back at him.

"Don't count on it," Caroline taunted them, skipping after them with a smile on her face. "I'm the biggest and the oldest, so I shall find the biggest and the best blackberries."

"I'm the smartest, so I will find the most," Emily pro-claimed, joining in the game.

"No you won't," Beatrice said with a scowl, rushing after them with her skirts in one fist and pulling Louisa along be-hind her. "I'm the fiercest and Louisa is the sweetest and nicest, so we will find the most. Won't we, Louisa?"

They were so busy arguing with each other and searching out the biggest and tastiest blackberries along the hedgerows they forgot about the rain and the cold and the hunger in their bellies. Mid-morning had come and gone before they wearied of the game.

Teddy, his hands and mouth dyed purple with blackberry juice, was the first to stop. "I've eaten so many blackberries I've got a stomachache," he announced proudly. "That means I won."

Not wanting to be outdone, Dorothea clutched at her own stomach. "I've got a stomachache, too."

Now that Caroline thought about it, her stomach wasn't feeling any too healthy, either. "We all won," she announced, "but Teddy and Dorothea won more than the rest of us," she added hurriedly at the look of belligerence she saw forming on two small faces.

They had, indeed, all won, as they were a good mile or two closer to the workhouse without even noticing the walk. Another couple of hours and they would be there.

It was closer even than she had thought. A half hour or so trudging along the lanes brought them to a small village. In the distance they could see the forbidding brick face of the workhouse, set apart from the respectable parts of town, looming above the humble cottages like a vast prison.

Now they were so close she could not bear to hurry there. Once the workhouse gates closed behind them, there would be no escape. "I need a rest," she pronounced, making her way over to the village green and plonking herself down on the grass.

The others followed her, subdued now that the end of their long walk was finally in sight.

The village bakery lay across the green, wafting the smell of fresh bread across the grass. Caroline's stomach rumbled. Blackberries were all very well in their place, but they didn't fill the belly like a good loaf of bread did. By the looks on their faces, the others were all thinking similar thoughts.

One of the villagers passed them as they sat there in silence, a curious look on her face. They must look a sight, Caroline thought uncomfortably, wincing inwardly at the woman's scrutiny and then chiding herself for her folly. At the workhouse they would have to get used to worse things than the stares of strangers.

The same woman passed them by again a few minutes

later. This time her curiosity got the better of her and she approached them cautiously. "I haven't seen you around before."

"We are just passing through," Caroline answered politely. "And we stopped for a rest."

"You needing anything?" the woman asked. "My son and daughter-in-law own the bakery over yonder. My boy makes the best yeast rolls in Christendom, if I say so myself."

Caroline felt her face go red. "Thank you, but we don't need anything. We have already eaten."

"We had blackberries for breakfast," Teddy piped up, showing off his purple fingers proudly. "I found the most."

"You're not still hungry?"

"I'm starving," Teddy admitted cheerfully. "Papa died so we have to go to the workhouse," he went on before Caroline could stop him. "Caroline says they will feed us there."

The woman's face softened. "I thought as much," she murmured to herself. "Poor wee mites, all dressed in black as they are." She reached into the bag she was carrying and drew out a large loaf. "Here, share this with your sisters," she said, pressing it into Teddy's hands. "It will keep you going until you get to the House."

Though Caroline's face was burning with shame, she did not have the heart to refuse the woman's kindly gesture. Her pride could bend just a little to fill the emptiness of Teddy's stomach. "Thank you," she said, almost choking over the words.

The woman gave her an understanding smile. "There's more of us than you'd guess who've had a stint in the House," she said quietly. "They treat you rough, but to give them their due, they feed you enough to keep body and soul together. I've had cause to be grateful to them more than once. Having to stay at the House for a time is not the end of the world."

Looking at the grim brick building in the distance, Caroline could feel no hope, no gratitude, for those who offered up this place of last refuge. There was nothing in her but blank despair. The workhouse was the end of her hopes, the end of her world.

Four

It was nigh on noon by the time they reached the tall gates of the workhouse. Her heart beating with trepidation, Caroline led them through and into the stone-flagged courtyard beyond. The courtyard itself was deserted, but she could hear sounds of industry in the distance—the muted clatter of breaking rocks and the thud of axe against tree. No voices, though. The world of the workhouse seemed to be inhabited by silent ghosts and machinery, not with living and breathing beings.

She looked around the courtyard, trying to get her bearings. Tall brick walls surrounded her on all sides so that she did not know which way to turn.

The workhouse was so big—larger by far than she had imagined it to be. Were there really that many poor people in her parish? She would not have thought there were half so many. Her hands shaking, she picked up the heavy brass knocker on the closest door and let it fall. It hit the door with a resounding clang that seemed to echo on forever.

Before the sound had completely died away the door opened and a thin-faced woman stuck her head out. "Visiting hours are ten till twelve on Fridays only," she said, and she made as if to shut the door again.

"We are not here to visit," Caroline said in a rush. "But to stay."

"To stay?" The thin-faced woman opened the door a little wider and looked them up and down with an assessing stare. "I haven't seen you before. Are you from this parish?" she asked suspiciously.

"From Bloomsbury," Caroline confirmed. It was the wealthiest part of the parish and would be home to few of the paupers in the House.

The woman's eyes narrowed at the name, and the door remained largely closed. "You don't look so destitute to me, with your fancy black clothes and boots and all. You sure you haven't come from one of those Welfare Societies to make trouble here?"

"Our father died, leaving more debts than we could pay. We have nothing."

"Hmmm." She pursed her lips as she opened the door a little wider and ushered them into a bleak waiting area with bare brick walls and a cold stone floor. "Come on in, then, and I'll ask the master to take a look at you. But don't say I didn't warn you if he finds out you're shamming. He won't treat you kindly."

Beatrice stepped forward as the woman was about to leave them again. "Can we have something to eat while we wait? We've been walking all day on only a few blackberries and a morsel of bread and my sister is not strong."

The woman gave a slightly malicious chuckle as she made her way to the door. "Dinner's over for the day. You'll have to wait till supper for a meal. That is, if the master lets you stay at all."

By the time the master of the workhouse arrived, the afternoon had almost disappeared into evening. Overcome with the twin effects of hunger and exhaustion, Teddy and Dorothea had eventually ceased their fretful quarreling, slumped onto the bare stone floor, and subsided into an uneasy sleep. Beatrice and Louisa sat at one end of the plain wooden bench that was the room's only furniture, their heads on each other's shoulders and their arms wrapped around one another, each one giving the other the only protection they could afford. Next to them sat Emily, her hands primly folded in her lap but her head lolling on one side and her mouth slightly open in sleep.

Only Caroline, squashed as she was at the far end the bench, and sick with apprehension over the coming interview with the assessor, felt no inclination to slumber. The blisters on her feet throbbed and the pain in her empty stomach was as sharp as the twist of a knife, but all her physical discomfort was nothing to the ache in her heart.

Her father—his greedy speculations and wild schemes to

double his fortune in no time at all—had made them sink so low. If only he had been content with all he had: a fine house, a fine family, and an income plenty large enough for all their needs. They had needed nothing more.

Just a few weeks ago she had loved him dearly. He had been her father, her protection from the world, even sometimes her friend. It was hard to remember that now, surrounded by her hungry and exhausted siblings and knowing that his greed and cowardice had brought them to such straits. And yet for all that, she could not hate him. It would be easier if she could.

No, her hate was centered on Captain Bellamy, on the man who could have rescued them all if he had chosen to. His mean, penny-pinching offer of keeping her was more insulting than anything else could ever be, more insulting even than the suspicious look on the face of the master of the workhouse who was now approaching her. He was a sandy-haired man of about her father's age, though with a rough, weather-beaten face that told of the hardships he had lived through, and a gammy leg that he supported with a stick.

"You're the ones who want emergency admittance?" he barked, his voice gruff. His sharp gaze took in the picture they made—wrinkled black gowns, unkempt hair, and pale, exhausted faces.

Caroline got to her blistered feet and dipped into an awkward curtsey. "We are."

He stopped in front of her, leaning heavily on his walking stick. "You're in fine clothes for paupers."

The sneer in his tone cut into Caroline's heart and brought tears into her eyes. If he did not take them in, they had nowhere else to go. "We have no others."

"Your parents? Where are they?"

"Both dead. My mother died ten years ago, when Teddy was born. My father...." She stopped to swallow the lump in her throat. "My father died just a few weeks ago."

"He left you nothing?"

"Only debts that we could never pay."

He looked them up and down critically. "You and your sisters look like strong enough lasses. Did you not think of looking for work instead of coming here to live off the generosity of your betters?"

She had not thought the bread of charity would be so bitter to the taste or so hard to stomach. "We were in mourning for the death of our father. By the time we realized what a state of desperation he had left us in, the bailiffs were in the house. They took everything. They would have taken the clothes off our back if they had not been too ashamed to turn us out into the street naked."

"You have no relatives to take you in? No grandparents, uncles, cousins?"

Did he think she had not scoured her memory and her father's papers for any trace of a relative who could be induced to take them? She could find no hint of any living relations on either side. "None."

"No friends?"

"None that would take in the impoverished brood of a bankrupt. No doubt they feared his ill-fortune was catching." She knew her bitterness was unjustified. Six additional people to feed, house, and clothe would be a huge burden for even the closest friend to willingly take on. She had not been able to bring herself to ask so much of any of her father's friends, and none of her own were in a position to assist her so much. Still, not to receive a single unsolicited offer of support was galling. When the chips were down, she had no one to depend on but herself.

"No other offers of support?"

The thought of Captain Bellamy set a nasty taste in her mouth. "None that I could accept."

His green-eyed gaze seemed to go straight through her, reading the secrets she did not confess. "You are proud for a pauper."

"I have nothing left but my pride. You cannot condemn me for holding onto that for as long as I can."

"Paupers cannot afford pride, lass." His voice was still sharp, but not unkind. "It's best that you learn that sooner rather than later."

She shrugged. Truth to tell, she had little enough of her pride left anyway.

"We'll take you in for now."

Her legs almost buckled under her with relief. Tonight they would sleep in a bed and not in a ditch. And they would eat. Her stomach rumbled loudly at the thought of food. "Thank you."

"We'll put you in the temporary section for the rest of the week. On Monday the Board of Governors will meet and they will decide in the end whether or not any or all of you will be allowed to stay."

A bed and food for the best part of a week was better than nothing. Surely the Board of Governors would take pity on their sad story and allow them to stay until she could think of a way to support them all. "Thank you."

"Don't get your hopes up," he warned. "The six of you look strong and fit and ready for work for the most part. The Board of Governors has little patience for able-bodied paupers and other malingerers. They are just as likely to toss you all out of doors again as give you free food and board for a day longer." He jerked his head at Teddy and Dorothea, who, their cheeks flushed with sleep, were slowly disentangling their clothes and sitting up on the floor. "Though they might make an exception for the two youngsters and keep them till they can be apprenticed out."

"You will let us stay until then?" How small her hopes and aspirations had fallen that she was thankful for so little.

"The last epidemic of cholera nigh on cleaned us out. Most of our inmates lacked the strength to fight it and half our beds are empty now. You may as well stay as not. Wait here and I will send the matron to see to you."

Caroline subsided onto the bench again as he limped out again. Could it possibly get any worse than to be grateful for a mere week in a cholera-infested workhouse?

★ ★ ★

The thin-faced woman who had opened the door to them bustled back into the room a short while later. "Come along with me. He says as you can stay for the week." She shooed them out the door, flapping her apron at them as if they were recalcitrant chickens. "Too softhearted for his own good, I'd say," she muttered under her breath as she led the way through a bleak, deserted courtyard and into a forbidding brick building on the far side.

Snaking their way through the corridors, they eventually came to a room with a bare stone floor in which stood a couple of tubs of water.

"Wash yourselves," the matron ordered brusquely, her hands squarely on her hips.

Caroline and her sisters looked at each other helplessly. The matron surely could not expect them to strip in front of her, and in front of each other, and wash themselves in a common tub.

She did expect it. "Hurry up. I haven't got all day," she snapped at them, as they did not move.

Beatrice stalked over and tested the water in the tub with the tip of her finger. "It's freezing cold," she stated. "And besides, it's dirty. You cannot mean for us to wash in that."

Caroline looked closer and saw the soap scum that lay on top of the water in the tub. Beatrice was right—the water was already filthy. They would not be the first people to bathe in it. The thought of sharing bathwater with the other inmates of the workhouse positively turned her stomach. Out of the corner of her eye she saw that Emily was looking as green as she felt.

"Take it or leave it—it's your choice—but nobody enters the workhouse without a bath. It's the rules. We don't want any vermin in here."

Caroline could not help but voice a shocked protest. "We don't have vermin."

The matron sniffed. "So all you paupers say. I never met a single one of you who wasn't fair crawling with lice and bugs. Now are you going to bathe or I am going to turn you out again?" The malice in her voice left Caroline in no doubt as to which option the matron would prefer.

Slowly, reluctantly, Caroline kicked off her boots and peeled her stockings off her blistered feet. What choice did they have? As far as she could see, they had none at all. If they did not bathe in that filthy water, they would not be allowed to stay. And if they could not stay, they would starve.

The stone flags of the floor chilled her feet to the bone but she did not hesitate. Discarding first her dress and then her chemise, she stepped over to one of the tubs.

"Don't forget yer bloomers," the matron cackled. "You've got to have a proper bath, mind. None of this wipe here and there with a washcloth and call yourself clean."

Her face burning, Caroline stepped out of her bloomers, kicking them over to the rest of her clothes.

The matron's cackle grew more throaty at the sight of Caroline's nakedness. "You've got pretty, white skin for a pauper, I'll say. Now, into the tub with you."

She climbed awkwardly into the tub, shivering as the cold of the water seeped into her bones. Taking hold of the coarse bar of yellow soap on the edge of the tub, she scrubbed herself all over as quickly as she could. Just as she was about to clamber out again, she felt the matron grab her head and push it under the water. Startled, she fought back until she surfaced again, spluttering and coughing out the water in her lungs.

"Yer hair needs washing, too," the matron said, taking the bar of soap and rubbing it roughly through Caroline's long hair, careless of the painful tugs she was administering.

Caroline's head was aching by the time the matron dunked her head a second time. This time, however, she was better prepared and managed to take a deep breath before being submerged in the water, and did not have to fight against the sensation of drowning.

"That's better," the matron said approvingly as she let her go again. "There's no use in fighting me." She showed her brawny arm off with pride. "There's not many women as can boast of a stronger arm or a harder fist than I have."

Privately Caroline thought the matron's brawny red arm was no cause for boasting to begin with, but she wisely held her tongue and clambered out of the bath in silence.

The matron tossed her a grimy towel, and she rubbed herself dry with relief. As she reached for her clothes again, the matron shook her head and snatched them away. "You can't wear those in here, missy. It's pauper's uniforms for you." She picked up a shapeless gray gown from a pile in the corner, held it up against herself and gave a nod of satisfaction. "That'll do." She passed it to Caroline. "Put this on."

Instinctively, she recoiled from the garment, this last indignity too much for her to swallow.

The fierce look returned to the matron's face. "What's the matter now?" she inquired acerbically. "Pauper clothes not good enough for you, are they?"

Caroline gestured toward her black gown. "Can we not wear our own clothes? Our father died."

"Hoity-toity for paupers, aren't you?" She thrust the gray gown at her. "Fathers die all the time and life goes on just the same for everyone else. All the workhouse folks wear these. I won't be making any exceptions for a brood of ill-mannered brats who haven't the grace to be thankful for the charity that keeps their body and soul together."

"But we are in mourning. We should not wear gray gowns. It is not respectful."

"Go naked then and see if I care." The matron cackled nastily. "I'm sure there are more than me who would like to look on your fresh, smooth skin."

Shivering with cold and silently apologizing to her father in her mind, Caroline took the gown and pulled it over her head. Every way she turned, she seemed to antagonize the matron. But to be refused the opportunity to pay her respects to her father's memory hurt worst of all—worse by far than the pain in her belly or the ache in her feet. She had spent her last pennies on outfitting them all appropriately in black, and now their sacrifice was to be in vain. They had been refused permission to wear the clothes that had cost them so dearly, and so her father would not be properly mourned. They had no relatives, no one who would wear black for him.

From another pile the matron drew out a pinny for Caroline to tie on top of her gown, a pair of coarse woolen stockings, and a couple of thick-soled work boots. "Mind you don't go getting your things dirty," she warned. "There's no clean clothes to be had until wash day."

Her heart sank still further. "When is wash day?"

"Every second Friday. Your clothes have to do until then."

So, they would not even have clean linen. Another indignity to strip away another tattered shred of pride.

"Now come along, the rest of you. I don't have all day."

Caroline turned and faced Teddy and her sisters. "That wasn't so bad," she lied, willing her teeth to stop chattering. The coarse linsey-woolsey of the gown scratched her skin, and the boots were a size too small and hurt her feet dreadfully, but for the sake of her sisters she had to put a brave face on it. Complaints would get them nowhere. They were paupers now—there was no use pretending otherwise.

One by one they all followed her example. There were tears in Louisa's eyes as she discarded her black gown, and Beatrice's scowl would have curdled all the milk in the dairy, but still they did as they were bid. Caroline heaved a sigh of relief that they had the sense to behave. Until she came up with a plan to earn enough money get them all out of the workhouse, like it or not, they were stuck there and had to abide by the same rules as everyone else.

The matron washed the others with brisk efficiency. When she came to Teddy her face softened momentarily. "Had a bonny boy myself, once," she remarked to no one in particular. "He's all grown up and gone for a soldier now. Writes to me once a month, regular as clockwork."

When they were all dressed, the girls in identical linsey-woolsey gowns and pinafores, and Teddy in a thick smock and coarse pants, the matron had them line up in front of her.

"Names and ages," she demanded, her thick black pencil hovering over a small book she had extracted from her pocket.

Caroline stepped forward to answer for all of them. "Caroline Clemens, nineteen. Emily, seventeen. Louisa, sixteen. Beatrice, fourteen. Dorothea, eleven. And Edward, ten."

"Sixteen and over gets put in the adult ward," the matron said absentmindedly as she scribbled in her notebook. "You'll be expected to pick oakum with the rest of the inmates, unless you're too weak or sick to work." She lifted her head from her notebook for a moment to glare at them. "A word of warning in case you are tempted to malinger—if you don't work, your food rations get cut. This is a workhouse, not a house of leisure. You must earn your keep here, same as you do on the outside.

"You two younger girls," she continued, pointing at Beatrice and Dorothea, "will go into the ward for young females, where you will be put to learning those skills that will help you to get along in the world. And the boy will be put with the other children."

A gasp of dismay escaped Beatrice. Her face had turned a pale shade of gray and she was holding onto Louisa's hand as if it were a lifeline. "Do you mean to separate us?"

The matron eyed them sternly. "You'll be allowed to visit each other once a month, if you behave yourselves and don't get into trouble."

"Once a month?" Caroline echoed Beatrice's gasp of horror. She had always thought that even if they were in the workhouse, they would at least be together. But what was the use of being incarcerated in the same place if they could only see each other once a month? Teddy would be all alone, without anyone to guide or comfort him. And how would Beatrice survive the separation from Louisa, when the two were so close they seldom spent more than an hour a day apart? Despite her seeming fragility, Louisa's will was as strong as steel, but poor Beatrice would crumble without her older sister. Beatrice had cultivated her strength in order to protect Louisa—without her, she would have no reason to keep going.

"Once a month and no more," the matron repeated sternly. "Assuming, of course, that the Board of Governors lets you stay at all, which is by no means a surety."

★ ★ ★

By the end of their first week in the workhouse, Caroline was almost hoping that the Board of Governors would not let them stay. Starving in the hedgerows could not be any worse than what they were forced to endure in this charitable institution. And at least in the hedgerows they would be all together.

Along with the other women, she and Emily and Louisa had been set to work picking oakum. The work was hard enough for hands already toughened by labor, but for the soft white hands of girls accustomed only to embroidery or painting, it was excruciating. After barely ten minutes picking at the tough rope, untwining the strands, Caroline's hands were rubbed raw. In less than an hour they were blistered and bleeding and so stiff he could barely stand to move them. The pain after a day's work kept her awake at night, tossing and turning in her narrow cot. Neither Emily nor Louisa fared any better. And, most worryingly, Louisa had started to cough in the night, a thin hacking cough that did not bode well.

Despite the pain in her hands, Caroline did not dare to stop. The food, even for the workers, was meager enough to leave her with a permanently hollow feeling in her belly. If her rations were to be cut, she would slowly start to starve. She had seen some of the inmates who were too sick to work, emaciated and hollow-eyed, wandering around the compound as noiselessly as if they were already ghosts. She did not want to join that company of the living dead—not while she still had a spark of life left in her.

She could only hope that Teddy and Dorothea would be

partially cushioned by their youth and their natural high spirits. And the young were not dealt with as harshly as the adults were. Once, she had seen from the window a group of children playing in the courtyard. Children were resilient, and Teddy and Dorothea were young enough to adjust. As long as they had enough food, and remained free of the cholera and the other diseases that haunted the workhouse, they would survive relatively unscathed until she had worked out a plan to free them all.

Beatrice, she was afraid, had already given up hope. Though they were forbidden to speak to each other except on their official monthly visit, Caroline had caught sight of her most days as the three older sisters were walked to the room where they picked oakum. Beatrice, more than any of them, had lost a lot of weight and looked positively haggard. More than her thinness, though, was the lack of spark in her eyes. No longer was she the defiant little spitfire who would take on the world to protect her beloved sister. Her spirit had broken under the harsh conditions and the separation from Louisa. Her shoulders slumped and her head was bowed, and her gaze followed Louisa with the hunger of a starving, abused puppy to whom food and shelter is only just out of reach.

Caroline made her way to the dining hall for their midday meal, her shoulders already slumping in exhaustion and her hands throbbing in agony. Beatrice, more than any of them, needed to be rescued. The workhouse was not the reprieve she had imagined it to be. It was nothing more than the beginning of a slow death. If she did not get them out, they would all rot and die there.

Just as she reached her place on the bench and sat down to eat, the matron stepped up and called out her name in a stentorian voice. She rose from her place and bent her head submissively. "Yes, Matron." She had learned early on that any sign of spirit was taken as a personal affront.

"The Board of Governors met this morning. You and your sisters and brother have been refused admittance. You must be on your way this afternoon."

She looked longingly down at her bowl of thin soup and the hunk of black bread and cheese on her plate. Even with this awful news ringing in her ears, her stomach clamored to be fed. "Refused?" Were they to be denied even this postponement of death? "But we have nowhere else to go."

"That's not what the Board of Governors said. They claimed you had turned down a perfectly unexceptional offer of support from one of your father's friends, a Captain Bellamy. The Captain himself confirmed that he had made such a gesture, and moreover swore that he was still willing to provide you with an establishment according to the terms of his original offer."

"Unexceptional?" Caroline's voice rose in dismay. "Did he fail to inform the Board of Governors that his offer came with strings attached? That it was not at all the sort of offer that a respectable woman could accept?"

The matron shrugged. "I don't care what sort of offer it

was. It's not my business, but the business of the Board of Governors. Orders is orders. Now come along."

Caroline stood her ground. There was nothing left for her to lose. "I want to see the master."

"He'll just tell you the same as me."

"Then he can tell me himself that he is refusing me and my sisters a place of refuge, and instead throwing us out onto the mercy of the world. That he is throwing us out so that the Captain can make a whore out of me." Despite her best efforts, her voice began to crack.

The matron shrugged. "Still just as hoity-toity as you were when you arrived, I see. Come with me and I'll tell the master as you wants to speak to him."

Hurriedly Caroline snatched her portion of bread and cheese from out of her bowl and hid it in her apron for later. Though it was strictly against the rules for any food to be removed from the dining hall, she was ravenous, and if she was to be thrown out on to the streets, heaven only knew when she would eat again.

The matron left her in the same echoing vestibule as when she first arrived. Caroline sat on the wooden bench and munched on her pilfered bread and cheese, making it last for as long as she could. Little as it was, it eased the hollowness of her belly and made her hunger bearable for a time.

A short time later she heard the telltale footsteps of the master limp down the wooden hallway. He stopped in the doorway. "You have heard already the Board of Governors has refused you admittance. What do you hope to gain from seeing me?"

At the look of resignation on his face, she knew at once that any protests she made would be useless, but still she had to try. "Captain Bellamy offered to make me his whore," she said bluntly. "That is the only support I can claim from him."

"The Board of Governors made no such mention of his intentions."

"Did you think he would tell them?" she asked bitterly. "Did you think he would make it widely known that he offered to corrupt a young woman of good morals? A woman to whom he had once been engaged, which engagement he cruelly and callously broke off in order to wed a wealthier woman?"

"The board has spoken. You have no right of appeal. And I cannot afford to have you stay and to feed you out of my own pocket. You would be taking food out of the mouths of your fellow inmates. I cannot allow that."

Her shoulders slumped. Thanks to Captain Bellamy's lies, even this last refuge was now denied them. "It is already afternoon and the night will be here soon. Let us stay the night at least. We will leave in the morning."

He looked doubtful.

"You can send the bill for our food and lodging to the Captain. He has offered to support us, hasn't he?" she asked bitterly. "He can pay for one more night."

Still he hesitated.

"And you have my leave to charge him enough to double everyone's rations for a week."

At that his face creased into a smile. "You drive a fair bargain, lass. You and your family can stay for tonight. But tomorrow you must leave."

"After breakfast." That at least would ensure they got one last meal before they left. "We cannot walk far on an empty stomach."

"After breakfast," he agreed.

And she was forced to be content with that.

Dominic poured a generous measure of port into his glass and passed the decanter around the table to the fellow next to him. He took a swig and put his glass down on the table again. The temptation to get happily plastered was great, if only to make the evening pass more quickly. The dinner party had been awful, the food barely passable and not at all to his taste, and the company interminably dreary. Worst of all, it would still be a good hour before he could politely make his excuses and escape. He'd only accepted the invitation in the first place in an effort to get out more in English society, to make some new acquaintances and find a place for himself among the City bankers. And to find out where Caroline Clemens had sequestered herself.

While he'd been away in the provinces, her father's house had been sold and Caroline had vanished off the face of the earth. Though he'd searched everywhere he could think of, he had not found a trace of her. He could only hope that someone among her old circle would know where she had gone. A young woman could not disappear into thin air. Especially not with half a dozen siblings in tow.

It hadn't taken him long to decide that he wouldn't bother to cultivate a closer friendship with most of the people present. Self-satisfied and smug, they feasted on course after course of turtle soup, quail, venison, and every other delicacy money could buy. As they stuffed their mouths full of rich food, they decried the evil life of the poor of London, who lacked the means to buy themselves a simple loaf of black bread for their dinner and were forced to steal to keep themselves from starving.

He'd made a couple of discreet inquiries of his neighbors during dinner as to the whereabouts of Caroline Clemens but they had heard nothing of her since her father's death and clearly cared nothing about her fate. There was nothing left to do but wait until he could rejoin the ladies in the drawing room and extend his inquiries to the rest of the company. It stood to reason that one day, one of her old acquaintances would know something of her.

Dominic took another sip of his port, idly listening to the chatter around the table, but not joining in, when a couple of words caught his attention.

". . . old Isaac Clemens's brats."

His ears pricked up. Was that Caroline they were talking about so disrespectfully at the other end of the table?

"Really?" asked a languid man with a pale face and long muttonchop whiskers with a yawn.

The first speaker, his host for the evening, a fat, florid man by the name of Bartles, whose waistcoat buttons strained to stay closed over his paunch, gave a great belly laugh. "As sure as I sit here. The oldest Clemens girl, what was her name? The one who was going to marry Bellamy until he called it off. Sensible man, that, to refuse to take a pauper to wife. I would've done the same."

"Caroline," supplied one of his neighbors helpfully.

"Yes, that's it. Caroline Clemens and all the rest of them. They sued for admittance to the Bloomsbury workhouse a week ago. You could've knocked me down with a feather when their names came up in the meeting this morning."

"And did you let them in?"

"Let them in? Certainly not. Old Isaac Clemens died leaving more honest men than me out of pocket. I'm not paying yet again to keep all his brats in the workhouse. They can go and find an honest job and get a decent wage for an honest day's work and not rely on charity."

His Caroline in the workhouse? His stomach roiled with the rich food and wine he had consumed at the thought that she had gone to bed hungry. Could it be that she had no money at all? No relatives to take her in? No one in the whole of London to lend her a helping hand?

The uncharitable Englishmen around the table had thrown

her and her sisters out to starve with as little concern as if they were a litter of unwanted kittens.

The languid man gave another bored yawn. "Did old Clemens really leave them with nothing?"

There was a chorus of tut-tuts from around the table.

"Careless."

"Improvident."

"Bad businessman in more ways that one."

"Besides, from what I heard," the fat man continued, "Bellamy offered to pension the girl off so he didn't have to marry her. Let him pay for her and all the rest of Clemens's brood to salve his conscience. I pay more than enough of my hard-earned cash to feed paupers as it is."

Dominic finally found his tongue. "Caroline Clemens is living at the workhouse in Bloomsbury?"

"She was until this morning. They will have thrown her out by now." His voice was fat with satisfaction. "With a father like hers, it's no more than she deserves."

Dominic pushed back his chair and stood up. He had the information he wanted now. Besides which, he could not stand another moment of his host's smug cruelty. To rejoice that Clemens's innocent family had fallen so low that they had sought out the workhouse as their only place of refuge was utterly vile. To rob her of even this last haven was unspeakable. "If you will all excuse me," he said, not caring to hide the disgust in his voice. "I find that urgent business has suddenly called me away."

His host looked up from the table, a look of dismay on his oily face. "Must you leave so soon? Before we have even brought up the railway investments I mentioned to you before? I have been anxious to discuss those with you for some days now. I thought that tonight would present the perfect opportunity for us to come to an agreement."

First butter me up with turtle soup and fine French claret and then try to fob off your worthless stocks on me, Dominic thought in a savage temper. He had seen the tactic many times before in India but had not thought to see it used with quite such a lack of finesse in the City. "I have decided against investing my money in those particular railway stocks," he said smoothly. "Now if you will excuse me, there is a young woman I believe who is in need of my help."

As his host's red face turned an unbecoming shade of green and he stuttered an incomprehensible protest, Dominic turned on his heel and stalked out of the door.

His peremptory rapping at the workhouse door eventually brought a sleepy-eyed woman shambling to the gates. The glare on her face faded as she took in his elegant suit and the carriage that stood just beyond the gate, and her muttered grumbles died away on the instant. "How can I help you, sir?" she asked, her voice now dripping with honey.

"Caroline Clemens. Where did she go?"

Her head shot up with surprise. "You've come for Caroline?"

"Her and the rest of her family. I gather they have been here for the last week. Bring them here to me."

Her face took on a knowing leer. "You're the Captain, then, wot's promised to support the young lady?"

He raised one eyebrow at her impertinence. So that rascal of a Captain was still sniffing around Caroline's skirts, was he? He would put a stop to that soon enough. "Now, if you please. It's getting late. I don't have any time to waste."

Caroline came awake reluctantly, the matron's hand shaking her mercilessly until she opened her eyes.

"Get up, do you hear. The Captain has come for you. He wants to see you this moment, down in the master's office."

The Captain? At his name she came awake on the instant. Had he come to gloat over her in her misery, or to see if she was desperate enough to accept his offer now?

Was she desperate enough to become his mistress in exchange for a mere pittance? She was hardly in a position to bargain with him for more, given how little she had now.

Two hundred pounds a year was not so very little after all. If they found a very small cottage in the country and grew their own vegetables and kept chickens, they would be able to live. Emily was clever enough to find a position as a governess close by, and who knows, when they were grown maybe one of the girls would find a husband.

She rolled over and buried her head in her hands. The

prospect of throwing herself on the mercy of the Captain still made her sick to the stomach, but how could she avoid it now? She would die of shame if she accepted his offer, but they would all die of hunger if she refused him. All she could do was put off her choice for a few more moments. "Go away," she mumbled, feigning a sleepiness she no longer felt. "I do not want to talk to him."

Relentlessly the matron pulled her out of bed. "But he wants to talk to you. Hurry along now and throw on your pinafore or I will take you down to him in your shift." She leered unpleasantly. "Not that he would mind, I'm sure, a red-blooded gentleman like him."

The effort of putting on her stockings and boots made Caroline's hands bleed anew. She grit her teeth through the pain. It seemed she had no choice but to go through this interview now, whether she liked it or not.

Once dressed, she followed the matron down the stairs and through the workhouse buildings to the master's office.

The matron ushered her inside with a whispered injunction not to bite the hand that fed her, then shut the door behind her.

Caroline's eyes were glued to the threadbare carpet on the floor. She could not look the Captain in the face. Let him see to what depths he had driven her. If he had any conscience at all, the sight of her ought to smite him.

"Caroline Clemens."

That was not the Captain's voice, but a rich baritone that

even now had the power to send a shiver of sheer pleasure down her spine. Slowly she raised her head, hardly able to believe the evidence in front of her eyes. "Mr. Savage? What on earth are you doing here?"

"Looking for you."

Five

Caroline was suddenly, horribly aware of the picture she must present: rough work clothes, unbrushed hair tied back with a piece of twine, cracked and bleeding hands, and a face lined with exhaustion and worry. She put her hands behind her back and straightened her shoulders. "Here I am," she said as bravely as she could. "So now what are you planning to do?"

"I am going to take you away from here. To take you home with me."

She stifled the leap of hope that burst painfully into her chest. His sudden appearance in the workhouse in the middle of the night, where she would least expect to see him, seemed to be the miracle she had been hoping for, the miracle that would save them all. "My sisters and brother are here with me. I will not leave them." She was pleased to note that her voice hardly wobbled at all. Whatever he was offering her, she would never desert them. If he was to be her miracle, he would have to rescue them all.

"I am not asking you to leave them." His voice was impatient. "They must all come, too. I have a carriage waiting outside."

Still she did not move. No one took in a whole family of paupers without getting something they wanted in exchange. "And what are you asking for in return?" It hardly mattered what he wanted—she would give him anything he liked and more. Hunger and desperation had brought her lower than she could ever have imagined.

His face creased into a wry smile. "Do you always look a gift horse in the mouth?" With one hand he reached out and stroked her tangled hair. "You were not so shy with me that evening in the conservatory, or so intent on examining my motives."

Her face flamed as she remembered how wantonly she had behaved with him, with no thought of asking for anything in return but the pleasure he could give her. "I am sure what you are proposing is less in the nature of a gift, and more in the nature of an exchange. I would rather know where I stood first as last." She had let him have her once for nothing, but she could not afford such luxuries now. If only he were to offer her two hundred pounds a year to be his mistress, she would be his willing slave. Better him than the Captain, for sure.

"You would stand here and bicker over terms with me?" He moved closer to her and clasped her hands in his.

Wincing with pain, she withdrew them hurriedly and hid them in her pockets so he could not see the mess they were in. They were not the hands of a pampered mistress.

Gently this time, he took them out of her pockets and turned them over, swearing under his breath when he saw their sorry state. "You can hardly stand with exhaustion and you need to see a doctor. If we must argue over the terms of your rescue, let it be when you are back to full strength."

She could feel her eyes fill with tears. "You are really going to take us away from here?" The reality of her escape was only just now beginning to sink in, making her light-headed and dizzy.

"I shall have the woman fetch your sisters and brother and we will leave right away."

"You will be kind to them?" she asked, suddenly feeling the horrors of the last week crash in on her, leaving her barely able to support herself on her two feet. "You will not abandon them?" If nothing else, she had to get his promise on this before she left with him.

"I will treat them as kindly as if they were my own family," he said. "I swear it."

She knew instinctively he was not the sort of man to lie to her. "Thank you." Then the blackness that she had kept at bay all week crept in on her and she clutched at his shoulders to keep herself standing upright. This time not even the pain in her hands could keep the darkness at bay.

The last thing she felt was the sensation of his strong arms around her, catching her and holding her safe as she crumpled.

The short carriage ride was nothing but a blurred memory of Teddy and Dorothea hugging her as if she might vanish into thin air if they let go of her for a moment, and of the sight of Beatrice's face, alive with happiness once again.

By the time the carriage pulled up outside Dominic's house in Russell Square, Caroline knew that she would suffer any indignity, any hurt to her pride, for the sake of keeping her family safe from the workhouse. She would be Dominic Savage's mistress and perform any debased act he might command of her if he would but pay her enough to take care of them all.

With Teddy holding onto one hand and Dorothea the other, she clambered painfully up the steps to the front door, her blisters rubbing with every step.

The butler's eyebrows almost disappeared into his hairline when he saw Dominic standing there with a collection of grubby paupers, but he said nothing. "Have the housekeeper make up some beds at once," Dominic instructed him as he strode down the hallway with Louisa in his arms. "We have some unexpected guests."

The rest of them followed as he led the way into a large sitting room with a merry fire at the grate.

Teddy was looking around him in awe. "Do you have any food in this house?" he asked.

"Teddy," Caroline scolded faintly, though privately she had been thinking along the same lines.

Dominic laid Louisa down onto a settee. "You're hungry?"

"I've been hungry for ever and ever," Teddy replied, holding his chapped hands up to the fire. "The workhouse didn't feed us much, and when I didn't eat it quickly enough, one of the bigger boys would steal it from me. Sometimes they stole nearly all my dinner before I got to have hardly a bite."

"I'm really hungry, too," Dorothea chimed in. "But nobody stole my dinner. I would have punched them in the nose if they'd tried."

"Dorothea," Caroline scolded, scandalized. Had their week in the workhouse already turned her youngest sister into an irredeemable savage?

"They would have deserved it," Dominic agreed soberly. "But no one will steal your dinner while you are here." He rang the bell, quietly instructing the servant who answered it to bring whatever food they had in the house to the sitting room at once.

The food, when it arrived a few minutes later, made Caroline's stomach growl in anticipation. Roast beef and Yorkshire pudding still warm from the oven, a loaf of thick-cut crusty bread, a dish of celery, and a huge apple tart with a jug of yellow custard.

They needed no urging to gather around the table and eat, balancing the plates on their knees and stuffing food into their mouths as fast as they could get it there.

The taste of roast beef rolled over Caroline's tongue like a caress. She could have kissed Dominic right there and then for the simple chance to quell the aching hunger in her belly. Lifting her head from her plate, she swallowed her mouthful in a hurry. "Thank you," she said, feeling dreadfully ungracious for falling on the food like a starving mongrel instead of waiting to thank him first.

"Don't talk," he commanded her. "Eat. It seems as though the workhouse tries to starve its guests to death."

"They did their best—"

"Eat," he repeated. "I don't want to hear another word from any of you until every scrap of food on the table is gone."

The mountain of food lasted an embarrassingly short time. When all of them, even Teddy, had finally eaten as much as they could, only one small piece of apple tart remained.

Dorothea looked at it longingly. "Can I take that with me in case I get hungry in the night?"

"Don't be greedy," Teddy scolded her under his breath. "That's all the food we have left. We can all share it for breakfast in the morning."

"Apple tart for breakfast?" Dominic shook his head. "That may do very well for ladies, but us men need better nourishment than that. I will ask Cook to make us ham and eggs and sausages and cold meat pies instead. Does that sound acceptable?"

Teddy's eyes had grown wide at the thought of eating so well again in the morning and he nodded.

"I want ham and eggs just like Teddy," Dorothea demanded, though her eyes still lingered on the apple pie. "And meat pies, too."

"We shall all have ham and eggs and pie for breakfast," Dominic agreed. "But I think now you need some hot water for washing and a clean bed to sleep in." He beckoned in the bevy of maids who stood waiting in the hallway. "Please, see our guests have everything they need."

As the younger ones trooped obediently out of the sitting room, he stayed Caroline with a hand on her arm. "Come with me. I will show you to your quarters myself."

Mutely she followed him up the stairs, wincing at the dusty marks that her boots left on the fine rugs. He led the way down the hall to an elegant bedroom done out in a beautiful shade of pale blue. "You can sleep here. I have asked the maids to bring you in a tub of hot water right away."

Her eyes were immediately drawn to the connecting door on one of the walls. She walked over to it and pushed it open. As she had suspected, it lead to another bedroom, one done out in a more masculine dark blue, and obviously inhabited. Now that her stomach was full and her faintness had passed, she felt well enough to carry on the conversation they had started in the workhouse. She might as well get the terms of his rescue out in the open sooner rather than later. It was better to know where she stood right away, and to bargain for the best terms she could extract from him while he still wanted her.

His offer to keep her, if she read his intentions rightly, might have insulted her a week ago, but she was beyond being insulted by such things now. Unlike the Captain, Dominic had never promised her any more, or offered to take her as his wife. Dominic was not expecting to be married to one of her old friends and wanting to set her up as his mistress at the same time, paid for by the money his wife would bring to him. If he would but settle a small sum on her, enough for them all to live on, and maybe even agree to give Teddy an education and help him off to a good start in life, she would accept him as her lover with alacrity.

While he was still pleased with her, she would save all her settlement to dower her sisters. They would never marry well, not with a whore as a sister, but if they could find somebody who would support them and be kind to them, what else would they really need?

Maybe she ought to be ashamed of herself, selling her body for so little, but she could find no shame in her soul. Only a bone-deep relief that maybe, just maybe, if she played her cards right, she had found a way to save her family. "What do you expect from me in exchange?"

For the first time that evening he looked uncomfortable. "You are tired. We should have this conversation in the morning."

"I would rather have it tonight, if you don't mind." She gave a small smile. "It is bad bargaining to accept the goods before you have settled on a price for them. Or to accept an offer to buy before the compensation has been discussed."

Just then there was a knock at the door and a footman entered with a large tub, followed by a procession of maids with huge kettles of hot water. "Our piped water would never cope with half a dozen baths in a row," he explained. "So I had some extra water heated on the stove for yours."

She looked longingly at the steaming water, torn between the desire to climb into the tub and the need to clarify her position in the household before she accepted any more favors from his hands.

"Go ahead and bathe while the water is hot," Dominic said. "We can talk in the morning."

Caroline looked at the steaming water, then at Dominic. Making a quick decision she hoped she would not live to regret, she drew her pinafore over her head. If she was to play the part of a mistress, she would play it to the best of her ability, and extract whatever concessions she could from her new keeper while he still wanted her badly. Right now, her sensuality was her only ally against starvation for all of them. It were best she used it to her advantage. "Don't go," she said as she tossed her pinafore on to the floor, removed her boots and stockings and wriggled out of her gown. "We can talk while I bathe. If you have no objection, of course."

★ ★ ★

Dominic swallowed uncomfortably. If he had no objection? For
hours he'd been thinking of nothing but getting her naked, of
running his hands over her creamy white thighs, of taking her
nipples into his mouth and sucking on them, and of plunging
into her tight, wet cunt and thrusting into her hard and fast,
riding her until she was as mindless with desire as he was. Seeing her collapse in front of him with worry and exhaustion,
watching her eat as if she were half starved, and knowing the
painful state of her hands, he'd deliberately tamped down his
desires.

She needed to eat and sleep, and then have a doctor tend to
her injuries. The last thing she needed was to be importuned
by a man who wanted nothing more than to taste her sweet
body again. If he were to have his way, there would be plenty
of time for him to taste her in the coming months. As much
time as he needed to take his fill of her.

But here she was right now, standing in front of him, as
naked as the day she was born, and asking him to stay and
converse with her as she bathed. He was a man, not a saint.
She was playing with fire. And by the calculating look in
her eyes, she was well aware of the danger she was in. There
was no way he was going to walk away from her now. He
had spent too many nights thinking about her, dreaming
about her naked body held against his, to resist her. "Be my
guest."

Gingerly she stepped into the bath, giving him a tantalizing view of her naked ass in the process. "Oooh, the water is hot," she said in a throaty voice as she sank down into the tub.

He knew exactly what she was doing—she was trying to play him like a fish on a line, to reel him in and ensure he had no wish to escape her net. He could even pinpoint the exact moment she had decided to do so, when the bath had arrived and in the space of a heartbeat her attitude changed from directness, even aggression, to sultry promise.

Her week in the workhouse had not broken her spirit, or turned her into a shrinking violet. Clearly she was still the brazen temptress who could seduce him in the conservatory at a soiree, who could tease and kiss and fuck him until he was utterly satiated, and then walk away from him without a single backward glance. He was beyond glad that her fighting spirit had remained intact. Violets had never been his favorite flower.

She had no need to reel him in—she had already caught him. At this moment, with her naked body just a few feet away, he would give half of what he owned to make her his. The Captain would never know what a fool he had been to give up such a woman for mere money.

"So, to our bargain," she said as she ran a cake of soap first along one arm and then the other, her voice as even as if she were talking about nothing more engrossing than the weather. "Exactly what are you proposing?"

"Your father left you with nothing."

A flash of anger crossed her eyes so briefly he wondered if he had imagined it. "As you see." Her voice was cold. No, he had not imagined her anger, though whether she was angry with her father's improvidence or with him for mentioning it, he could not tell.

"I am a wealthy man."

She let her gaze roam pointedly around the rich furnishings of the bedroom. "So I see."

The knowledge of her nakedness beat an insistent tattoo in his blood. Grabbing a chair, he pulled it over to the tub, positioning it so he could stare openly at her nakedness. "And I want you." In her pauper's dress, she had been a delicious morsel. In the bath, she looked like one of the irresistible sirens of old who had tempted sailors to a watery death on the rocky reefs that surrounded their island country.

Her back arched, making her nipples break the surface of the water. "As I recall, you have already had me."

"Ah, yes, the conservatory." The memory of their first lovemaking flooded in on him with a rush, making him stand fully at attention. Damn it, but the woman was a tease. Surely she had to be fully aware of how she was affecting him and was doing it on purpose.

"Exactly."

"That was only a nibble to whet my appetite. I'm still hungry. I want the full banquet."

"You want a good deal."

"I am prepared to pay well for my pleasures."

A flicker of distaste crossed her face. Though she had begun it, she did not like this bargaining with her body. She had not been born to be a whore, exchanging pleasure for money. Still, he admired her for making use of her one remaining asset to ensure a future for her family.

"How well?"

She had been generous to him in the conservatory, giving herself to him without a thought of taking anything from him but pleasure. Now it was his turn to show her that he could be generous, too. "I will settle a sum of five hundred pounds a year on you." He could easily afford it, and such a sum, though not wildly extravagant, would keep her in decent comfort. She would never have to beg for her bread again.

Her face paled and she gave a hiss of indrawn breath. "That is generous of you." Her voice shook just a little as the enormity of what he was offering sank into her brain.

But he hadn't finished yet. "You will have the town house at your disposal for as long as you choose to live there. I will send Teddy to school, and any of your sisters who wish it. They will each have one thousand pounds for a dowry to enable them to marry respectable men, and Teddy shall have the same to help him enter a profession."

As he spoke, she gradually recovered her composure. "And if I were to ... if we were to ..." Her face reddened and her voice tailed off into embarrassed silence.

He divined what she had been too shy to mention. "And if we were to be blessed with children, I would acknowledge them and support them while I was alive, and they would have a goodly share in my estate when I am gone."

Her gaze held his. "And what will you expect from me in return?"

He had never noticed before what a glorious shade of brown her eyes were—deep and clear, with a hint of gold in the very middle. "In return, you will be my lover, my mistress, and mine alone. You will take no other man to your bed, indeed you will scarcely look at another man without my express permission. You will belong to me, body and soul." Those were his terms. He would take nothing less.

Perching one leg on the rim of the tub, she soaped along its length. "Do you expect your five hundred pounds a year to buy you a slave?" Her voice was calm enough, but he could hear a definite spark of interest in it. She was not put off by his terms, not at all. The thought of being his slave excited her.

"Not only a slave, but a willing slave," he clarified. "I expect that my money will buy me a woman who will spend her days thinking up new ways to please me, and her nights putting her ideas to the test. A woman who will travel on a sensual journey with me, as eager to taste and feel and experience everything as I am. A woman who will not only willingly lift her skirts for me to fuck her in the conservatory at a fancy party, but who will beg me to take her to places she has never been before.

"I do not want a corpse lying underneath me on the bed, mutely accepting whatever indignity I may perform on her. I expect my five hundred pounds a year will buy me a woman who will be an active and eager participant in our lovemaking, open to teaching and being taught. A woman who will be endlessly accommodating and wildly inventive, a woman who will endeavor to match me in every way."

"You want me to *want* to sleep with you." She paused in the act of soaping her other leg and tried, unsuccessfully, to hide her shiver. "All the money in England could not buy a woman's desire."

"Did you couple with me in the conservatory because I was wealthy? Or because you wanted me?"

She turned her head away from him with a pout. "I was upset. You were there."

How delightfully transparent she was, and virginally shame-faced about enjoying the pleasures of the flesh with him. "Do not lie to yourself. You wanted me. If you are to accept my offer and become my lover, I will not allow you to lie, either to yourself or to me, about your desire for me. I would have you shout it from the rooftops."

She turned back to him, her face wearing a mulish expression. "And if I do not accept, what then? Will you throw us all back onto the streets tomorrow morning without ceremony? You cannot take us back to the workhouse. They will not take us back—they had already given us notice we had to leave in the morning."

There was no question of her refusing him. He would not take no for an answer. One way or another, she would be his. "I would not throw you into the streets, no. Not even a dog deserves to lead such a life as that."

"You would not throw us out?" The disbelief and cynicism in her voice belonged to someone twice her age.

"I would not throw you out. But neither would I feel inclined to treat you with as much generosity as I would treat my lover," he added with brutal honesty. "I would see that you and your older sisters obtained suitable employment, and Teddy and the younger girls were given apprenticeships that would, in time, enable them to support themselves. I would do that much for anyone in your situation."

All trace of the sultry temptress was gone, making way for the practical businesswoman that lurked just below the surface. "Employment?"

She need not think she could escape him that easily. He had not rescued her so she could be a governess in another man's household. Still, she might as well believe that she had a choice in the matter. She would take to the life he had planned for her more easily if she believed it was the life she had chosen for herself. "As a nursery maid or a housekeeper, or even a governess, if your education were to prove up to the challenge. The lad could be sent to the counting houses. They could no doubt use him there."

Her face fell. "We would be separated, then."

To be good at bargaining, she would have to learn how to

hide her emotions better. "That is the lot of plenty of families too poor to stay together," he said casually. "You would at least survive."

She nibbled on one fingernail. "If I were to become your mistress, you would send Teddy to school?"

"To Eton, if he liked it."

"And help him to enter whichever profession he chose? The army? The clergy? Law?"

"Naturally he would have the choice. I would help him in whichever way he needed it."

Her face had brightened with every answer he gave her. "And dower all my sisters?"

"With a thousand pounds apiece."

Her forehead creased into a frown. "A thousand pounds is little enough inducement for an honest man to marry the sister of a whore."

"It is a thousand more than they would otherwise have," he pointed out.

"It's not at all certain that any of them will ever marry, and then all your promises will cost you nothing. Make it fifteen hundred each and give them a sporting chance."

He revised his earlier opinion of her astuteness. She wasn't too bad a bargainer after all. "Twelve hundred and not a penny more."

"Twelve hundred then." A triumphant smile spread over her face at the agreement they had reached. "But it must be signed, sealed, and agreed to in front of witnesses."

There was no doubt about it—she was a very sensible

young woman. "I will have my lawyer draw up the papers in the morning."

"And one last thing." She hesitated before she spoke again. "My father was a successful man, until one foolish investment ruined him. I do not mean to insult you or your business acumen, but I do not wish to trust my future to a speculator, even as successful a one as you seem to be."

She did not trust a speculator? He raised his eyebrows, waiting to see what was coming.

"I want the capital to fulfill all your promises lodged safely in the Bank of England. I dare not risk losing everything all over again."

For the first time, her request gave him cause for concern. "You do not know what you are asking for." He ran his hands through his hair. He'd never considered she would make such an unusual demand of him. Lodging such a vast amount of money in the Bank of England would seriously cut into his working capital.

"On the contrary, I know exactly what I am asking," she replied a little stiffly. "You are asking me to become your mistress. In doing so, I lose my reputation and become a courtesan, which is nothing more than a fancy term for a common whore. All I am asking in return is that you ensure that you are able to hold up your end of the bargain."

He could feel his temper rise with every word she spoke. All his dealings were honest and aboveboard. He did not deserve her mistrust. "I would never cheat you."

"I trust you would not intend to. Just as my father did not intend to lose all his money and end up bankrupted and disgraced."

Making over a certain amount of income a year was one thing; setting aside the capital to generate that income was quite another. Much as he wanted her, he would not let her lead him around by the nose. "I cannot afford to make over such a capital sum. Not all at once. It would cripple my business dealings."

"Then I will be a governess." She shot him a sidelong glance from under her lashes. "Maybe I will have the good fortune to work for a lonely widower who is looking for a wife and isn't fussed about a dowry. Or maybe one of my employers, or one of their friends, will be a wealthy rake and will be able to set me up as I deserve. I am sure I will study to make it worth their while."

The thought of her studying his wants, his desires, seeking to please him in all things, made him stand to attention even straighter in his trousers. He'd tasted her once, and their encounter had given him a yen for her that demanded to be satisfied. She knew it, too, the little witch, lying back in her bath, stark naked and unashamed, daring him to turn his back on her and leave her for another man. By God, but he would not let her go now, to have her innocence despoiled by some aristocratic rake who would use her and discard her with as little thought as if she were an embroidered handkerchief made to wipe his nose on.

He did a few rapid calculations in his head. "I can't do it. I don't have the ready money to deposit."

"Then I had best brush up on my French and my dancing so I can find a good position. Do you dance?" The sultry look in her eyes hinted at the kind of dancing she wanted from a man. "Will you dance with me until I find an employer? One who can recompense me as I deserve?"

He had never waltzed in his life, but he'd dance the shaking of the sheets with her any day. "But I do have a small property in Hertfordshire that brings me in about four hundred a year," he said, as an idea occurred to him that might keep both of them happy. "The yield could perhaps be increased with close management. I could make that over to you, if that would meet your needs." Giving away the land would not hurt his business interests as tying up his business capital would.

Her eyes lit with interest. "A small property? You would make over some land to me?"

"I have no sentimental attachment to it. In fact, I've never even seen it. It was given to me as part payment of a debt and brings me in what was promised, so I have never bothered with it." He pulled a wry face. "I am a railway speculator, not a farmer. I know nothing of sheep and pigs and cows."

Her whole body was brimming with excitement. "That would take care of your obligations to me, but what of Teddy's profession? And my sisters' dowries?"

He had her now. She was going to accept his offer. "They will have to rely on a speculator's promises. I will pay them when they wed. Not before."

He could almost see the wheels clicking around in her head as she weighed up her options. Eventually she gave a quick, decisive nod. "I will accept the property, then. I will be your mistress, and will study to be everything you ever dreamed of."

Caroline sank back into the bath, letting the cooling water flow over her body. It was decided. She would be a courtesan, a woman who used her body to entice men, to drive them so wild with desire that they would support her in comfort, even in luxury. Her stomach turned over, bile rising in her throat. She only hoped she would be up to the challenge.

Dominic would not be too much of a problem, at least at first. It was clear he already desired her. Enough to make over a small property to her.

She hugged her exultation close to her chest. A small property was even better than money in the bank to her—when Dominic eventually tired of her, her family would have somewhere to go. They could all live in the house as well as draw an income from the farmlands. She only hoped he did not tire of her too soon, but considered her worth the extortionate price she had demanded of him.

Slowly she rose from the bath, her wet hair dripping down her shoulders. "Pass me a towel, if you please." They had struck a fair bargain. Now it was time to pay the piper.

Though she had agreed to be a whore, she was an honest one and would fulfill her end of the bargain to the best of her abilities.

His eyes were smoky with desire as he stepped toward her, towel in hand.

She held out her hand, trying to stop herself from blushing or turning away at his open scrutiny of her body. A real courtesan would not be embarrassed at her nakedness. A real courtesan, she was sure, would use it to drive her protector wilder than ever with desire, so he would not tire of her. "The towel."

His face had a feral glint in the gaslight. "I do not think so."

The chill of the night air was forming goose bumps on her wet body, and her nipples had formed into tight, hard buds with the cold. "Please." Now was not the time for teasing her.

Stepping closer, he stroked down one of her shoulders with the towel. "Why should you have to dry yourself when I am here to do it for you?"

His light touch heated her chilled body from the inside out. She would not have been surprised to see tendrils of steam rising from her damp skin. "You do not have to act as my servant."

"I am not acting as your servant but as your lover." His words flowed over her like rich chocolate as he ran the towel over each shoulder and arm, over the planes of her back and the peaks of her breasts. "A lover tends to his mistress's needs just as she tends to his. And your need at this moment is to be warmed and dried."

"I am quite warm now," she protested. The goose bumps on her arms were gone, but her nipples were peaked harder and tighter than before. Too much warmer and she would begin to drip and melt right back into the bathwater again.

His eyes lit up with a knowing smile. "Good."

The satisfaction in his voice made her squirm. It was as if he could read her thoughts, could read her desire for him and the need that he made her feel. "The fire is very warm," she said stoutly. One thing she knew for sure about her new profession was that she could not afford to be weak, or to let her desires overrule her good sense. She must drive men wild for her, until they would pay any sum of money, give her any-thing, for the delights of tasting her. Allowing any man, espe-cially Dominic, to turn the tables on her and to make her fond of him was the beginning of the end. Her affections would make her vulnerable, and she could not afford any weakness. Her family depended on her. Their welfare had to remain at the forefront of her mind.

Still he stroked her with the towel, though she was sure she was as dry as dust already. "You desire me," he said. "You want me to take you again, to fuck you like I did in the conser-vatory. You should not try to pretend otherwise. That is not the bargain we have made."

It was true. Her knees were weak and her breath came short with wanting him. She wanted him to take her again, to brand her with his ownership, to make her feel alive. She could not hide her desire from him. It was foolish to think that she could.

Lusting after him did not have to be problem, though. Every animal felt lust and an urge to procreate. As long as she remembered that teasing him and pleasing him was her profession now, and had nothing to do with softer feelings of liking, or even, God forbid, love, she would survive.

Sexual desire was her meal ticket—her desire as well as his. She would foster his liking for her, and draw him on by showing him how much she wanted him. Surely he would want to feel irresistible, to have his good opinion of himself flattered. That would make him want her all the more, maybe even fall a little in love with her. Yes, if she could manage to make him fall in love with her, then her future would be assured. If he was genuinely fond of her, he would surely treat her well and be generous to her, more generous than if he simply wanted to fuck her.

Love, however, was her enemy. She would have no truck with love at all.

She held out her arms to him and allowed him to pat her injured hands dry. "I cannot touch you as I would wish to," she said, looking ruefully down at the deep cracks and weeping blisters that marred her palms.

His brows drew together in a frown. "I will have a doctor see to those in the morning."

"Can he see Louisa, too?" All thoughts of being seductive

flew out of her mind as she thought of her sister's worrying cough. "And Emily's hands are worse than mine."

"He will see Louisa, too. And Emily. And anyone else who needs him. I will ensure he is at your disposal for the whole day, or longer if you would like."

"Thank you." She blinked back the tears that threatened to spill down her cheeks. He was a good man to look after her sisters with such thoughtfulness, and she was grateful to him. Even courtesans were allowed to feel gratitude. How different he was from the miserly Captain Bellamy. And what a lucky escape she'd had not to be wed to Bellamy.

He reached out and drew his fingers over her cheeks. "Don't cry."

"You are very good to us."

"I am investing a lot of money to have you at my disposal. There is little point in leaving you unhappy when investing just a little more will put a smile on your pretty face."

His words, kind as they were, recalled her to her duties. "You deserve to be thanked properly."

"Properly?"

She dropped to her knees in front of him, a smile flitting across her face. "Or improperly, if you would prefer." Ever since their interlude in the conservatory, she had been secretly longing to examine him more closely. Being Dominic's official mistress was going to have its advantages.

His groin was at eye level now and the bulge in his trousers was unmistakable. She reached to unbutton his trousers and then winced with pain. Maybe not. "Unbutton your trousers for me," she demanded. She might not be able to use her hands very well, but there were other things she could use to give him pleasure. He had showed her how that night in the conservatory. Now seemed like a good time to put his lessons into practice.

His fingers hesitated over the buttons. "Are you sure?"

Her face grew hot with shame as she rocked back on her heels, away from him. Had she read his mood wrongly? "Do you not want me?"

"I am not a demanding master." His voice sounded choked. "We will have plenty of time for you to fulfill our bargain. Tonight you are tired and have been half starved. And your hands hurt."

Is that all that was bothering him? That she would think he was too demanding? She leaned closer in to him and breathed on the bulge in his groin, pleased to see it twitch and grow still further with desire for her. "I wasn't going to use my hands." Seeing him stand in front of her, swollen with wanting her, gave her a feeling almost of power over him. He was her master and she was bound to obey him in all their sensual games, but she was not helpless, either. She could make him desire her, whether he wanted to or not. Once she had him in her mouth, all his self-control would not avail him, and then, when he lost his control and was mindless with need for her, she would have the upper hand in the games they played.

His hands moved over his buttons and he began slowly to

undo them. She could make out no expression on his face, it was as blank as if he were in a trance.

His trousers once undone, he attended to the placket of his drawers, drawing out his swollen cock with a sigh almost of pain. His trousers and his drawers fell around his ankles. With a muttered curse, he pulled off his boots and tossed them into a corner, then stepped out of his pants and kicked them over on top of his boots. Wearing nothing but his linen shirt and waistcoat he stood in front of her, mutely begging her to touch him.

She drew in a hasty breath at the sight of his huge cock, moving her head back from his swaying erection. Surely it was bigger even than it had been in the conservatory. Or had she simply failed to do it justice in her memory?

Her hands might be sore, but that would not stop her from giving him pleasure. With the tip of her tongue she tentatively licked up and down its length, over the ridges and dents, down to the base of the shaft and then up again to the massive purple head. A drop of fluid leaked out of the eye at the top and she licked it away, savoring the salty taste of his masculinity.

"Take me in your mouth. Please." His words were a groan and his hands tangled in her hair, urging her forward onto him. "I've been dreaming about this for so damn long. I can't wait any longer."

She shuffled forward on her knees until she was at his feet, taking him deep into her mouth as she did so, caressing him with her tongue and lips and bringing a groan of pleasure to his lips.

The towel on the floor kept her knees from the cold, and the bathtub against her back steadied her from falling over as he thrust his hips at her mouth, as eagerly as if she had already stripped away his last vestige of humanity and he was nothing more than a brute with only bestial instincts left to him.

His lack of control heated her body even more than the hot bathwater had. She felt a rash of warmth spread out over her chest, and in between her legs she felt a rush of liquid. Her body was getting ready to welcome his cock where it belonged, deep inside of her. She rubbed her thighs together, trying to slake the desire that was building up inside of her, but the friction only made it climb higher.

Her nipples were peaked to tiny nubs of desire. Leaning in closer to him, she touched them against his bare legs. The hairs on his legs tickled them and made them still tighter.

Wanting to excite him as much as she could, she decided to play the submissive further. She held her hands behind her back, giving the impression of being tied and helpless. And as a bonus it hid her ugly, injured cracked hands from sight. Spreading her legs slightly she lowered her body so her head was below the level of his cock. Then she looked up to catch his eye, encouraging him to enjoy the view of her body.

With her hands at her back, her breasts thrust forward, and her head tilted back to look up at him, she gave a light lick on the underside of his cock. "Does my master desire me?"

She rubbed her sensitive nipples against his legs overtly, swaying from side to side, and all the while looking up past his cock to meet his gaze. His face was tight, pained, as if he were only just managing to hold onto his self-control. "Would my master like me to caress him like this?"

Her tongue tasted his sac, tight in the cool air. With each tantalizing lick his cock gave a little spasm. He didn't have to reply for her to know that he wanted her. She could feel his back arching, his cock thrusting, encouraging her to continue.

His growing desire excited her in turn. She could feel herself growing even wetter between her legs. Her parts were burning for him, wanting his touch. She longed to touch herself, but resisted, keeping her hands behind her back. This was for him, not for her.

Shifting up a little, she once more took him into her mouth, touching him only with her lips on his cock. Moving her head back and forth she pleasured him with her mouth, pausing occasionally to swirl her tongue over the swollen head.

The touch of her tongue made him moan in delight. And when she added a gentle suction, pulling him greedily into her mouth and only reluctantly letting him go again, his moans grew almost painful.

Although she was playing the part of the mistress and he was her master, she was certain it was she who was in control.

How far would he go for her? What was the extent of the

power she could wield over him by acting as his slave? She looked up at him once more. "I cannot touch you with my own hands, but I would like to see you pleasure yourself, to see your hand at your own cock, then taste your seed as you cry in pleasure. What would my master say to that?" That way he could find the release he needed without the guilt of demanding her full participation.

There was only the briefest of pauses. "I could do that. But I would want to look at you as I did so."

Though he had tried to keep the emotion out of his voice, she could tell the idea of touching himself in front of her excited him. She wondered nervously which view of her he would enjoy the most. She could lie on her back and display herself openly for him, or she could remain on her knees and turn around, providing him with a fine view of her from the back.

The former, she decided. That way she would be able to watch him, too.

Pulling away from, him she lay on her back, continuing the fiction of being bound by keeping her injured hands behind her. Hesitantly she spread her legs wide and raised her knees. She could do this. Despite her relative innocence, she could play the part of an experienced courtesan. There was too much at stake for her to fail. "Does my master like this view?" she asked shyly. "Can he see my wetness? Can he see how I desire him so?"

He stood over her for a moment, then came down to kneel

astride her stomach, one hand wrapped around the base of his cock. Looking her in the eye, he rubbed the tip of his cock over each of her nipples until they were hard and tight, then moved up to rest his cock at her mouth.

When she lifted her head slightly to taste him, he backed away, teasing her. "Ah no. You shall not get any pleasure from this yet, my dear mistress. This is for me alone."

Moving back a little he began to move his hand rhythmically along the full length of his hard shaft, first slowly, then faster as his breathing quickened.

When his breath was coming in short pants, he slowed his pace, changing to short strokes near the base. He let his cock bob tantalizingly before her for a moment while he teased his own nipples. Each time he pinched them, his cock jumped a little, seemingly getting bigger and harder with every spasm.

Beneath him, Caroline watched as he touched himself. Never in her wildest of thoughts would she have ever imagined seeing such a sight as a man pleasing himself. But oh, how erotic it was.

She felt as if she were on fire. Desperate to do more than simply watch, she surreptitiously rubbed her legs together to ease the ache building up inside her. Her desire was stronger even than it had been in the conservatory. If she did not get some release soon, she was going to die.

Once more he took hold of himself and again grazed over her nipples, teasing the hard points with the delicate head. His touch was feather light, but it burned her like molten lead.

Resuming the full strokes, he rose up a little so his balls swayed just above her mouth, his pumping hand directly in her line of sight. Gingerly she lifted her head to lick his sac, egging him on with little cries of pleasure.

He was nearing completion, she could tell. His balls became tight and hard, his tempo increased, and his chest flushed with the impending release.

Suddenly he cried out, buckling over as his cock spurted across her breasts. He straightened as a second stream of milky white fluid jetted out over her lips and chin. Finally, with a loud cry, one last long spurt of his seed covered her breasts in stickiness.

Exhausted, he collapsed onto her, spreading his seed around farther and getting half onto his own chest in the process. He kissed her, not at all afraid of his own taste.

"You will make me a good mistress, Caroline. You will not regret the bargain we have just sealed."

She would not regret their bargain, not when it gave her his protection. Though she was his mistress, she was her own woman. She would not allow him any other hold over her. "I will do my best to please you."

As if he read her thoughts, he got up from her and kneeled beside her. "Spread your legs a little."

She complied silently, and he put his hand to the top of her pussy and began to rub her swollen nub. It was only a short while before it was her turn for her breath to come in short pants, her own breasts to flush with pleasure.

Her orgasm built quickly, then peaked as she cried out, her back arching with the intensity of the moment. There she hung, her body locked in orgasmic paralysis until slowly her senses returned and she collapsed exhausted to the bed.

She had given him pleasure and he had returned the favor. There was nothing else to the moment they had shared. Nothing at all.

Six

The following morning Caroline sat at the breakfast table with her family, her stomach full of ham and eggs and muffins, and a steaming cup of coffee cradled in her bandaged hands. Dominic had already left for his office in the City, for which she was grateful. Telling her siblings of her decision was better done in private.

Sipping on the scalding hot coffee to give her courage, she announced baldly, "I have agreed to become Mr. Savage's mistress. In return he will support us all."

"You knew him before, then?" Emily asked. "I confess I have been wondering why he chose to rescue us—and what he wanted from us in return."

"I had met him once, briefly, on the same night the Captain broke his engagement to me. I had not thought his interest in me was anything more than a passing whim." She gave a wry smile. "I still don't know whether it is anything more than that. But he is at least willing to pay handsomely to satisfy his whims."

There was silence for a moment and then Emily set down her knife and fork and looked guiltily into her face. "Thank you, Caroline." Her ears were pink and Caroline could read the shame in her eyes. "I, for one, do not have the selflessness to turn down the sacrifice you are making for all our sakes. All of us owe you more than we can ever repay."

Caroline's heart hurt. She did not deserve their thanks. "You don't know what you are saying. I am no longer a respectable woman. I have sold my body for money, the same as any poor wretch on the streets. I am a gay girl, a whore."

"Caroline, you should not say such words," Teddy broke in, scandalized. "Nurse would wash your mouth out with soap if she heard you."

Caroline shrugged. "You see what I mean? You will all be tainted by association with me. You girls will never make good marriages."

"You think some man would take us to wife from the workhouse?" Emily asked with a sniff. "You have not spoiled our marriage prospects any worse than they were already. If it had not been for Mr. Savage, we would all have died in the workhouse. I would have made the same bargain as you, if Mr. Savage had offered it to me."

"All of you, Teddy most of all, will have to suffer taunts about the way of life I have chosen. Taunts that you will not be able to refute, because they will all be true."

"If anyone says bad things about you and Mr. Savage, I will punch them in the nose," Dorothea put in. "That will teach them better manners. Mr. Savage gave us all apple pie."

Caroline bit back a smile. "Ladies do not talk about punching people in the nose. And they certainly do not ever hit anyone, no matter how badly they are provoked."

Dorothea pouted. "Then I will not be a lady. I will be a boy like Teddy and then I can punch anyone I like."

"Life will not be easy for you with me as your sister." Caroline took a deep breath to give herself the courage to propose what she knew would be best for them to accept. "I have been thinking that maybe it would be for the best if you were to publicly disown me and distance yourself from me. I would still support you, of course," she added hastily, "but you would be free to make your own way in society without me as a millstone around your necks. My name could be rightfully forgotten."

There was a general gasp of denial. Louisa was the first to speak. "You have rescued us from hell on earth, Caroline. We would all have done the same if we could. I would never turn my back on you, not even for show. Not even if it meant I could marry the Crown Prince himself." Even those few words brought on another fit of coughing that left her gasping for breath.

The others all nodded in agreement.

Their unwavering support brought tears into Caroline's eyes. It was more than she had hoped for. "Thank you. It means more to me than I can say that you will back me in the life I have chosen."

"You only do it for us," Louisa said, her coughing fit having subsided. "We are grateful to you."

"The life of a kept woman is precarious," Caroline warned them. "I will not always be able to support you as well as I can now. Mr. Savage will eventually lose interest in me and I will have to find another protector who may not be as rich or as generous as he is. You would be wise to take advantage of his generosity while you can, and prepare yourself to earn your own living. I would not have you face the same choice that I have had to make."

Emily poured herself another cup of tea. "You are right. It is not well done of us all to rely on you for longer than we must. As for me, I have always fancied being a teacher in a girls' school. I will look for a place nearby that will take me on for a trial, with a position at the end of it if I prove to be useful." She sipped her tea thoughtfully. "Maybe Mr. Savage would write me a recommendation if I were to ask him. My French is fairly dreadful, to be sure, but my mathematics is excellent. And I can teach the piano and the harp, too."

Much as she hated the idea of Emily leaving them to work in a school, Caroline knew that being a teacher would be a good occupation for her. It was an honorable profession and Emily was certainly clever enough to teach a whole class full of young girls. Though she wouldn't ever be wealthy, such a career would at least keep her away from the poorhouse.

Selfishly, she was only too aware that the sooner her siblings were self-sufficient, the easier it would be for her. If her sisters were all assured of a future, she would not feel constrained by poverty to take on a protector that her soul revolted against. As long as they were all cared for, when Dominic tired of her she could simply retire to the country and into obscurity on the money from her property. Such a life would suit her very well.

Louisa sighed. "Best of all I would like to be a mother and have a whole pile of children of my own, but if I cannot do that, then I will be a teacher, too. A teacher in a nursery school, though, so I can look after the little children. I will not need much training for that, but I will need a good recommendation, I should expect, to find a position."

Caroline felt for her younger sister. Just like Louisa, she, too, wanted what she would never have—a husband and children of her own. "It is not what we were brought up to expect, I know, but it is better than the workhouse."

Louisa gave a telling shudder. "Anything is better than that."

"I should like to be a nurse," Beatrice said stoutly. "That way I can look after Louisa when she gets ill. I'm sure Mr. Savage will be able to find a doctor who will take me on to train me in what I need to know. I do not want to learn any more French or music or other silly stuff. I would far rather be an apprentice and learn something useful."

"I will go for a soldier," Teddy said. "I will wear a red coat and be the bravest soldier in the whole army and bring you home a whole pocketful of medals."

"Me too," Dorothea added. "I will be the other bravest soldier in the army."

"Girls cannot be soldiers, silly," Teddy scoffed. "Only boys can be."

Dorothea's self-confidence was not punctured in the least. "Then I shall be a pirate instead. I shall be the captain of a pirate ship and I shall make all my captives walk the plank. And when I catch you, I shall make you walk the plank, too, so you splash into the water and spoil your red soldier's coat. Then you will be sorry I couldn't be a soldier instead."

Teddy's face got a mulish look. "I won't walk the plank."

"I will have a big sword and I will make you."

"Will not."

"Will too."

"Teddy and Dorothea, please." Caroline fixed them both with a glare until their squabbling subsided. "There will be plenty of time later on for you to decide what you want to be. In the meantime you will both be sent to school."

They groaned in unison at the prospect and only recovered their equanimity when Caroline helped them both to their third plate of ham and eggs for the morning.

Dominic worked fast. Anxious to have Caroline to himself as soon as he could, he put his considerable talents to work finding suitable employment for her sisters. With a few sums judiciously paid to smooth his way, Dorothea and Teddy were quickly settled in new schools close by, Emily was found a position as a trainee teacher at an exclusive girls' school in Hampstead, and Louisa and Beatrice were settled together in the household of a prominent London doctor—Louisa as their nursery governess and Beatrice as the doctor's assistant nurse.

Louisa and Beatrice were the last to leave. Their bags in one hand, filled with new clothes and all the other little necessities of life, they waved good-bye, climbed into the carriage and were off.

Caroline stood at the front steps, a tear in her eye to see them go, and watched the carriage as it turned the corner and rattled out of sight.

Dominic put one arm around her shoulders to comfort her. Though it was for the best that they leave to make their own lives, he knew she would miss them terribly. "They have not gone far. Just to North London. None of them have gone far. You will be able to have them here to visit every Sunday."

Swallowing back her tears, she nodded. "This Sunday?"

He leaned over and licked away the tear that rolled down her cheek, not caring who could see him. Now that her family was gone, she belonged entirely to him. How he had been looking forward to commanding all her time and all her attention. Now she could properly fulfill the terms of their bargain without any other cares to interfere with her duties to him. "This Sunday." His mind was already racing ahead to plan all the ways he could spend the rest of the week with her until then.

With a slight pressure on her shoulders, he led her back into the house.

"You have been good to my family."

Her gratitude gave him an uncomfortable feeling in the pit of his stomach. He had only been generous to her because he wanted her in his bed, and that was the quickest and most painless way of getting her there that he could think of. Under his tutelage, she would repay him for every penny he had spent on her, and more.

Heat coursed through his veins at the thought that finally she was his and his alone, and ready to be taught all the sensual games that he had learned in India, all the games that pleased and excited him beyond measure. The people of India were famous for their sensuality. They had created the *Kama Sutra*, after all, and he would explore every page of it with a willing and submissive Caroline. Though he'd had to pay for her subjugation to his every whim, still, her willingness was all that he had dreamed of finding.

"There's little point in having a mistress with a long face," he said offhandedly. "If you would rather have a few hundred pounds in school fees rather than the same in jewelry, what difference does it make to me?"

"It makes a big difference to me."

By now he had led her into the parlor and seated her next to him on the sofa. "Then may I suggest you show me your gratitude in a way that I will appreciate." He'd waited so long to have her all to himself—he didn't want to waste another minute of the time they had together.

"What would you like me to do?"

"Kissing me would be a good start."

After a moment's hesitation she leaned over and pecked him on the cheek. "Thank you."

Her breath was soft and sweet and the innocent caress went straight to his groin. He shifted uncomfortably. Thank heavens his house was his own again and he could be assured of an undisturbed afternoon. "That wasn't quite what I meant."

Her eyes, when they met his gaze, were completely guileless. "What did you want, then?"

"I want you to take off your clothes, Caroline."

Her face paled and her whole body went as still as a statue. "Here? Now?"

"You have agreed to be my mistress, haven't you?" he inquired silkily.

She nodded. "I have."

"And you have also agreed to be my willing mistress, to do exactly as you are bid with cheerful alacrity, to explore the limits of your sensuality with me, haven't you?"

"I have."

"Then why the hesitation in complying with such a simple request?"

Still she hesitated. "I had not thought you would want me

during the day. In the parlor. When the servants might come in at any moment to stoke the fire."

"You might have considered that before you agreed to my terms." Her innocence was working on him like a powerful aphrodisiac. Did she really think a man would only lust after his mistress in the dark of the night, when they were abed together? "It is too late for you to change them now."

She swallowed and her fingers moved to the buttons on her bodice.

"That's better," he said approvingly. "I like to see your cheerful obedience." He leaned back on the sofa, watching her through hooded eyes as she discarded her clothing, piece by piece.

As each item fell away, she moved more slowly, clearly hoping for an instruction to stop. He did not give her one. The languidness of her movements and her unconscious grace aroused him as much as the increasing amount of bare skin she was showing.

By the time she had stripped to her chemise, she was moving with glacial speed. Instead of taking off her shift, she plopped herself on his knees, straddling his lap, facing him. "Am I naked enough for you yet?"

Her bottom pressed into his groin, making his erection nestle snugly in the juncture of her thighs. He lifted the hem of her chemise to stroke her firm white legs. "Not by a long way."

"You want me to take off my shift as well? To have me naked on your lap?" Her voice was breathy and she arched her back, making her breasts sway tantalizingly under his nose.

His tongue snaked out to wet his lips. "I want you naked. Take off your shift."

"Don't you want to do it for me?"

"No. I want to watch you."

"Then, as you are my lord and master, I suppose I will have to oblige you." She wriggled about on his lap far more than she needed to free the hem of her chemise and then drew it up her thighs a little way. "The fire is too far away. I will be cold with no shift on."

"I will warm you."

"You promise?"

"I promise."

She wriggled her shift up a little higher, displaying the merest glimpse of her nest of curls. The sight made his mouth grow dry. Though he'd had her in his bed every night since she moved into his town house, this was the first time he had seen her naked in the daylight. The bright sunshine displayed her better than any dim gaslight or firelight ever did. He could gaze on her for hours at a time and never tire of the sight of her naked beauty.

He reached out and brushed her soft curls with the back of his hand. She shivered at the touch and drew her shift up a fraction higher.

Suddenly he lost patience with her games. He wanted to see all of her. Right now. "Take it off," he commanded.

"As you please." She drew the shift straight over her head, her breasts thrusting into his face as she stretched backward.

He captured one of her nipples with his mouth, tugging on it to keep her back arched.

Scooting her down on his lap a little, with one hand he fumbled with the buttons on his breeches. He undid them only enough to let his cock spring free. "Sit on me. Take me inside you."

Obediently she stood up, still straddling him. Her pussy left a patch of wet on his trouser legs, letting him know that despite all her protests, she wanted him as much as he wanted her. He took her hand and placed it on his hard flesh. With one soft hand on his eager cock, she guided him to the entrance of her cunt. And then slowly, oh, so slowly, she sat down on him.

She was as wet as London in the spring, and infinitely hotter. With his hands on her hips, he guided her to slide up and down on his shaft until her breath started to come in little pants and her eyes closed in passion.

She was about to come. He could feel her excitement from the first tentative tremors that were beginning to engulf her. But it wasn't enough for him. He wanted to claim her, to brand her with his ownership.

He slid her off, holding her back from sitting down on him as she struggled to impale herself on his hard length once more.

He rose from the chair, taking in her flushed face and the

smoky desire in her eyes. God, but she was precious to him. She was more than he had dreamed of, more beautiful, more accommodating, more luscious, more of everything than he could want her to be. "Turn around," he instructed her. "I want to take you from behind."

Dazed with unfulfilled lust, she was malleable as clay in his hands. With a few swift movements he arranged her as he wanted her, bent over at the waist with her elbows resting on the sofa and her legs wide apart.

Instinctively she thrust her bottom up in the air, making her cunt gape wide. He ran his fingers over her pink flesh, loving the silky wetness of her on his fingers.

She moved against his fingers, demanding more than the light touch of his hand. She wanted him inside her again, pounding her to the heights of pleasure.

His lust was demanding exactly that. With a firm hand he guided his cock to her entrance and then, with a long, fast thrust, he sank deep, deep into her.

With a gasp she arched back to meet him, urging him on.

Wet and tight, she closed around him like a sheath. Only the prospect of sinking back into her allowed him to draw out of her.

Her body clung to his as if she did not want to be parted, even for so short a time as this.

With his hands on her hips, he held her still, thrusting in and out of her with deep strokes that caressed him from the root to the tip. Her softness enveloped him, urged him on.

Reaching around her, he took her full breasts in his hands, squeezing them tightly as he thrust into her.

She was his. No one else's but his. No other man had grasped her breasts in his hands as he took her against the sofa. No other man had seen her naked skin, white in the soft afternoon light, as she writhed under him.

He was still as hard as stone, harder than he had ever been. With Caroline in his arms, he felt like a king. He wanted to keep on pleasuring her for hours, with long, slow strokes that reached into her very soul.

He felt the tremors in her pussy that signaled her pleasure was not far away. Sinking deeply into her, he held himself deep inside, moving slightly from side to side to allow her to wring out the last drop of pleasure from his position.

One more long slow thrust and she could no longer hold out against the tide that swept over her.

Her tremors brought him close to the brink. Anchoring himself tightly with his hands on her hips again, he thrust into her with short, fast strokes until he felt his cum rise to the top of his cock. Then, with one last thrust, he buried himself inside her as his cum spurted out in hot jets of ecstasy.

Careless of the stains on his velvet sofa, he fell back onto it, pulling her on top of him.

Lying back on the sofa, Caroline entwined in his arms, he could think of nowhere else he would rather be. When he was with Caroline, he thought only of her. She had chased the ghost of Maya from his thoughts.

He would never forget his first wife and the happiness she had given him. Still, she had been gone for three years and more. It was past time the pain of remembering her faded from a white-hot shaft to a dull ache.

He had been right to follow his instincts and take a new woman to his bed. Possessing Caroline had helped the pain of losing Maya to fade. Thanks to his new mistress, his soul was his own once again.

The days passed pleasantly enough for Caroline in her new life as Dominic's mistress. Being a fallen woman was not as dreadful as she had feared it might be. Most of the time, in fact, it was perfectly pleasant.

Dominic went into the City each day to conduct his business, leaving her at leisure to spend her days as she pleased. She had fewer duties than even when her father was alive. Then, she had run the household and done the household accounts. As Dominic's mistress, she could hardly interfere with the running of his household, despite quickly learning that the cook was a drunkard who stole spirits out of Dominic's cupboard and the housekeeper was such a tartar to the underservants that none of them would stay for more than six months at a time.

Her sisters quickly settled into their new lives, and though they visited every Sunday as they had promised, the rest of the week she spent largely alone. Her chosen profession having banished her from respectable society, she was completely cut off from her old circle of friends and acquaintances. She could have spent her days shopping for new clothes and other baubles, but after outfitting herself and her sisters with the necessaries, she no longer visited the shops. Tempting as it sometimes was to spend the bright guineas that weighed down her purse, her newfound independence was not going to be squandered on fashionable walking dresses, fur muffs, and other fripperies.

Besides, the joy of shopping was not worth the shame she felt when she ran into Captain Bellamy walking down Oxford Street with a blushing Kitty on his arm. She had turned away and pretended not to see them, but not before registering Kitty's gasp of shock and the Captain's avaricious leer.

All in all, it was easier to get her exercise walking in the gated park in the middle of the square where she lived with Dominic, admiring the babies in their prams pushed by smart-looking nursemaids, and avoiding the embarrassment of coming across old acquaintances or making new ones. When she was tired of walking in the park, there were always the financial newspapers that Dominic read over breakfast to amuse her, Mrs. Oliphant's latest novel from the lending library for light entertainment, and her correspondence with the manager of her new property in Hertfordshire to keep her busy.

And in the afternoon it was time to dress for dinner and make herself ready before Dominic came home. As her role demanded, she spent each afternoon thinking up new ways to amuse and entertain him, transforming herself in the evening into a saucy wanton whose only thought was to tease and seduce him. Though she now had half a dozen pretty dinner dresses he'd bought for her, best of all he liked to find her dressed only in a light Chinese-style robe, her hair loose about her shoulders and her feet bare. More than anything else, it excited him to return home to find her waiting for him, her loose clothing artfully arranged so the merest touch from his fingers would brush it aside.

Many evenings they did not even make it to the dinner table the servants had so carefully set for them, but went straight to bed together. He was always hungry for her, and she was equally so for him. The merest touch of his hand on her naked skin could make her shake with wanting him, and she soon learned how to raise and satisfy his appetite. Learning how to please him was no hardship. She delighted in having him under her spell and making him want her more fiercely with every day that passed.

After she had slaked his hunger for her, they would eat their evening meal at a small table in the bedchamber Dominic had placed there for that purpose. The rumpled sheets on the bed gave ample testimony to their activity when the poker-faced footman brought up their food, but he never gave any indication that anything was amiss. Her father's servants would have been scandalized, but Dominic's took their master's strange behavior in their stride.

Despite her evening games with Dominic, and her gratitude for being rescued from the workhouse, her life was quiet and lonely. When Dominic proposed one evening to take a holiday from his business endeavors and take her off on the train for a trip to Cornwall, she was delighted at the prospect and fell wholeheartedly in with his plans.

A week in Cornwall where she would not have to worry about meeting old acquaintances in the street, where she could be totally anonymous, sounded wonderful. And in Cornwall Dominic would be with her every day instead of just in the evening and at night. She had only seen one side of him, the side that burned to possess her. But in Cornwall they could not spend all their time abed together. She would get to know the Dominic of the daytime, Dominic the hard-headed busi-nessman, instead of just knowing Dominic the lover.

The railway station, a grand brick building with a tiled floor, was filled with more people than Caroline had seen gathered in one place before. Everywhere there were people on the move, going this way and that, jostling each other out of the way, each of them bent on their own business. Businessmen dressed in suits, with a briefcase in one hand and an umbrella in the other, hurried out of the trains as they steamed into the station and disappeared off the platforms toward the City. A group of ragged urchins played at marbles in one corner, now and then running shrieking among the crowd in search of an errant marble. Flower sellers hung around the pillars with baskets of fresh violets and pansies, calling out for pennies.

Dominic stopped to buy a posy and pinned it onto Caroline's bodice. "Flowers for my flower," he said, raising her gloved hand to his lips in the middle of the crowd. Before she could reply, he tugged her back into the milling crowd and through to the platform.

It was quieter there, with none of the bustle and hurry of the main station. Gradually Caroline relaxed and began to enjoy herself.

"Good day, ma'am. Good day, sir. 'Ave a pleasant journey." The guard in the guard's van had treated them like royalty as Dominic gave directions to have their luggage stowed.

Like a real married couple they strolled arm in arm up to the locomotive at the head of the train. It was ten minutes yet before the scheduled departure, and Dominic wanted to have a look at the steam engine, given his interest in all things mechanical.

She refused to dwell on the fact that they were not a real married couple. A courtesan did not care about marriage—it was too commonplace and ordinary, too middle-class for one such as her. She stifled the traitorous feelings inside her that whispered quietly of her need for love and affection. She was a well-paid courtesan, and that was more than enough for her.

He stopped in front of the engine and simply stared at it with undisguised delight. "It's not just a machine—it's alive. It's a huge dragon, spitting fire. A dragon that men have created and brought to life."

Caroline's excitement in making this trip was momentarily turned to awe when confronted with the huge machine. While not at all interested in the mechanics of trains, she had to admit to herself that Dominic's words did have a certain truth to them. The engine did almost seem alive as it breathed steam and smoke, occasionally even speaking with little clicks as various valves opened and closed.

Afraid of getting oil on her pretty traveling dress, she stood back from the locomotive as the engineers brought up the head of steam, the pressure venting more frequently as the time to leave approached. Momentarily letting go of her hand, Dominic walked up and down, looking closely at the components of the engine, in particular the steam pistons that drove the train at speed down the track all the way to Cornwall without rest or pause.

Her fingers strayed to the posy on her bodice as she watched him poke his nose into the noisy, smelly machine. He was just like a small boy, taking delight in the inner workings of the thing. The locomotive was like a new toy.

Just as she was his toy, she thought with a rare burst of anger at both him and her situation, to use as he pleased and then to discard when he tired of her. He had spoken the truth in calling her his flower. She would provide him with a transient moment of pleasure before she wilted to insignificance.

Returning to her side, he let loose his exuberance about being so close to the hissing engine. "Isn't it a marvel? That human ingenuity can design and build such a thing is a wonder. Just think about the changes railroads and the machines that run on them have wrought. England is more prosperous now than ever before." He shook his head in amazement. "What will the next hundred years bring? Flying through the skies in ships of the air, that's for certain."

His enthusiastic monologue was brought to a halt as the conductor blew his whistle. "All aboard!"

She threw off her black mood with an effort of will. She had known all along where she stood with Dominic—there was no sense in letting it upset her now.

Dominic led them briskly back along the length of the train to the second to last carriage. This carriage was painted differently than the others, and had expensive looking lace curtains over the windows. She followed him up the few steps and stepped inside, where she gasped in amazement. What her eyes beheld was not the rows of seats of a second class carriage, nor even the comfortable compartments of first class. The whole carriage was decorated like the study of a grand house, with a large desk, books, armchairs, and couches.

Dominic was looking very smug indeed at her surprise. "This carriage belongs to a business acquaintance of mine, a Mr. Gareth Hughes. He has close business ties to the railways, and in fact it was he who suggested we take a break at the house we are traveling to. He visited there about a year ago, and since then it seems his life and business dealings have been touched by good fortune. He was kind enough to offer this carriage to us for the journey."

Caroline walked around the carriage in delight, examining the fine furniture and furnishings until a loud whistle signaled that the train was getting underway. If she was his toy, she was at least a treasured plaything, and he treated her well. She had no real cause for complaint about her lot.

Their journey started with a jolt as the couplings joining the carriages took up the load, causing Caroline to stumble backward into his arms.

He took the opportunity to hold her close, while in turn she was in no hurry to break the impromptu embrace, treasuring the simple affection he gave her. "Oh, Dominic, it's lovely. What a simply decadent way to travel. I think I shall enjoy the journey as much as I shall enjoy the holiday itself."

He nuzzled into the back of her neck. "I have plans for you to enjoy this journey very much indeed," he murmured, sending a frisson of excitement down her spine. Was he really intending what she suspected he was? Was he going to make love to her in their own private railway carriage, with paying passengers mere inches away in the carriages on either side of them, oblivious to their shenanigans? The thought was so naughty, but so delicious, that her nipples tightened and she felt herself growing wet with anticipation.

The carriage rocked strongly from side to side as the train crossed over a series of switches, causing the couple to stumble to the nearest couch, where they landed in an untidy, laughing heap. As luck would have it, Dominic landed on top, pinning her with his weight—not that she had any intention of fighting him off. Quite the opposite in fact as she lay there laughing, happy for the moment to stop thinking of the past or worry about the future. For the next few hours the journey of her life would match the journey of the train, unable to change direction even if it wanted to. So, she decided, it was best to enjoy the ride and worry about the future tomorrow.

They lay together in companionable silence for a moment, their bodies rocking in time with the train, before Dominic released her from his weight. Walking over to a cabinet, he opened the door to reveal all manner of wines, ports, and sherries. Sitting on the shelf was an ice bucket with a bottle of champagne resting in a bed of ice. He opened the bottle carefully, so as not to allow the cork to fly around the carriage, then filled two crystal glasses and passed one to her.

"A toast," he said. "To us."

Seven

"To us," she chorused, taking a large sip. As the glass left her lips the unsteady carriage jolted once more, splashing the contents of her glass over her. With a start she jumped up and held the glass away from her, but it was too late. The wine had splashed her bodice, soaking through to her underclothes.

She swore under her breath as she looked down in dismay at the dress. "I'm afraid it's ruined."

"I'm sure we can arrange to have it cleaned. Duck into the water closet and take your wet things off. Then we'll see what we can do."

Once in the water closet, she removed her dress, opened the door just enough, and handed it out. Hiding in the closet, she waited with an ear to the door while Dominic summoned a steward and had him take her dress away for cleaning.

"Come on out," he called as soon as the carriage door shut behind the man. "There's no one here but you and me."

She looked down at her silk chemise and skimpy lace pantalettes that barely covered her knees. "But I am wearing only my underclothes." They were her favorite underclothes, true, but she could hardly wear nothing else all the way to Cornwall.

"This is a private carriage. I have locked the door, it's quite safe to come out."

Still she hesitated. "I feel too silly. What on earth would the conductor think if he were to see me half dressed like this traveling on a train?"

"Well, wait a minute."

There was a pause while Caroline heard the rustling of clothes. He must be arranging a replacement dress, or at least a dressing gown, she thought, though goodness knows how he could manage to do that on a train in the middle of nowhere.

"Right-o. You can come out now."

She opened the door to find no dressing gown, but Dominic quite naked. She gave a startled squeak to see his cock was half erect as he stood there in broad daylight, grinning that grin of his, completely unashamed. "Well, are you coming out?"

Caroline paused a moment while she considered her options. She could hardly hide in the water closet all the way to Cornwall. While proper ladies most certainly did not walk into the arms of a naked man whilst on a train, courtesans surely did, and she was a courtesan now.

And he did have a fine cock.

Not that she had much experience in other men's cocks, of course, but she did find his shape pleasing. Particularly when it was coming to attention as it was now, showing her just how much he wanted her, letting her know that he would not be forsaking her any time soon. She liked the confirmation it gave her without any words being spoken between them. As long as she could make him rise to attention like that, he belonged to her.

As she stared, his cock twitched and jumped a little, each time getting a bit harder, a bit more erect.

He held out his arms to her. "Come and kiss me, Caroline of the lacy pantalettes."

Still she hesitated. There were windows in the carriage. Would people in the stations as they passed not be able to see them?

"We will not be interrupted, I assure you. The doors are locked. You are safe."

Doing as she was bid, she hesitantly left the relative safety of the water closet and went to him. He took her in his arms, drawing her instantly into a deep kiss.

As she kissed him on the lips, she felt a gentle pressure on her shoulders, encouraging her to kiss him lower down. With his now very hard erection pressing against her midriff, her remaining uncertainty crumbled. She hardly cared anymore if people could see through the carriage windows. Let them look if they chose, she would not be ashamed. It was her duty to please Dominic, to keep him interested in her for as long as she was able. If he wanted her to suck on him on the train, then she would obey.

With one hand she held his erection, moving ever so slightly up and down, massaging him until he gave an almost imperceptible groan. At the sound, her hand movement grew harder and faster. She liked knowing that he enjoyed her touch. It made her happy to know that even though she had been his mistress for some weeks now, and even though she was still a novice at her trade, she could still make him want her.

Lowering her head, she kissed, then lightly bit and sucked on one nipple of his smooth chest. Turning her attentions to his other nipple, she teased them both into little hard points. Each time she nipped with her teeth, his cock jumped in her hand.

Continuing to lightly stroke him, she kissed her way down his chest, pausing for a moment at his navel until her tongue flicked lightly on the tip of his cock. Encouraged by his little moans of pleasure, with her other hand she lightly massaged his balls, gently feeling each egg shape in turn. They were soft and yet firm at the same time, giving way only a certain amount under her fingers, and covered with a sac that slipped and slid over them as if oiled.

Finally she could not wait a moment longer. She had to

taste him, take him into her mouth and suckle on him as he wanted. With her other hand still massaging the base of his cock, she took him into her mouth, savoring the velvet texture and salty taste of the purplish head with swirls of her tongue. As the train rocked back and forth, he slid in and out of her mouth in time with the movement.

After a few minutes of her suckling on him, he pulled away from her. "Too much of this and our lovemaking will come to a premature and explosive finish."

She looked up at him, disappointed, wanting him back in her mouth again. "And that would be a bad thing?"

"I need to taste you in my turn, to run my tongue into your wet opening, to tease the exquisitely sensitive place just above. And then, if you wish it, you will feel me deep in your pussy."

His words, and the tingling in her nether regions that they created, convinced her. She took one last lick as he pulled away from her mouth and knelt on the carriage floor in front of her. "Hold your arms up for me."

Her chemise was soon disposed of, over her head. Then her lacy pantalettes were slipped down over her hips and ankles. She made no move to stop him, as anxious now to be as naked as he was, and to have him licking at her as he had promised, and then sinking deeply into her.

Desire, she had found to her cost, was a double-edged sword. In making him want her, he had made her want him just as badly. She wasn't altogether sure that she always kept the upper hand in their lovemaking. Certainly, if he were to pull away from her now and treat her with coldness or disdain, she would weep.

But for now she need not fret. He was looking at her nakedness as if she were the most precious thing in the world and he had the job of taking care of her.

The train rattled on, green fields and hedges racing past the windows as fast as a horse could gallop, while inside the carriage she knelt naked on the rug. Her nipples had hardened into tight peaks, though she was not in the least bit cold. She felt deliciously aroused to be so exposed, in the daylight, in a carriage rocking its way to Cornwall.

Dominic had a wicked look in his eye. "Let me show you something new."

She eyed him askance. Was being naked in a carriage on a train not new enough for him? What else did he have on his mind? "Something you learned in India?" she asked suspiciously. She was wary of what he might have learned in that faraway place, where people were not even properly English, but burned brown by the sun.

"Yes, I learned it in India. They are masters of sensual pleasure, I assure you. This is something so sexy, so enticing, you will cry in pleasure within minutes, I promise."

She looked up into his eyes, kneeling there on the floor of the train carriage. Though her mind was uncertain, her body was on fire. Besides, it was her duty to obey him in whatever he wanted. "What do you want me to do?"

"Stay there kneeling, but move your legs apart a bit."

She did as she was bid, moving her knees until her pussy gaped open.

He lay down on the floor, head between her legs. His breath came hot on her and she almost came with the wet heat of it. He was going to lick her in this position, just as he had promised. She felt herself begin to drip in earnest with the anticipation of his touch.

Reaching up, he held her hips and pulled her down onto his face. She spread her legs farther, allowing him to make contact with his tongue.

He lapped gently at her, causing her to arch her back in pleasure and cry out, just as he had promised.

Moving her hips around, she discovered she could control where his tongue went. Maybe India had its good points, she conceded to herself as she whimpered with the enjoyment of it. First she shifted back to let him lick at her wet opening, then she moved forward a bit so he returned to that spot just behind. She wanted more. How she wanted more. And yet she wanted to continue in this position forever, with his tongue teasing and tormenting her until she died with desire.

She looked down at his cock, so very hard and twitching of its own accord. Surely he would want to taste some of the pleasure he was giving her. She could lick him as he licked her, and their double enjoyment would increase the pleasure fourfold.

Leaning over, she took the tip of him into her mouth, tentatively at first, then with increasing eagerness. His licking intensified as he rewarded her for her actions. Wrapping her hand round the base of his cock, she took as much of him into her mouth as she could, swirling her tongue around the head, then teasing the very tip.

With his hands on her ass, she felt him open her to his gaze. He wriggled a bit, and she felt his lips kissing her, sucking at the tender nub that gave her so much pleasure. The pleasure was almost unbearable as he continued to lick and suck on her. She could feel herself getting close to spending. Her breath came in short pants as she struggled to hold her orgasm at bay.

Then she felt a finger gently probing at her asshole, gently massaging the sensitive opening and dipping a little inside. She would never have thought she would enjoy such an invasion, but she did.

She pumped the base of his cock, her tongue lapping on the tender underside of the swollen head. Her pleasure was building rapidly with the combined attentions of his mouth and fingers. When she could no longer hold it back, she straightened up, pressing down on his face as her muscles began to lock uncontrollably.

Then, to her disappointment, Dominic stopped, pushing her to an upright position.

"Stay there." With those brief words he shifted up so his cock was near her opening. "Now, sit on me."

Caroline raised her hips a little and slowly lowered herself onto his erection until he was inside her as far as she could take him. He stretched her, filling her completely. "Is this something else you learned in India?"

"There is a famous book in India called the *Kama Sutra*. I was lucky enough to be given a copy, translated into English by one of our countrymen. Among other matters, it includes descriptions of various positions for giving and taking pleasure. This is one of the Perfumed Garden positions it describes."

Perfumed Gardens and books listing various positions for making love? India was climbing higher and higher in her estimation. "There are more than this one?"

"There are many more to try if you wish."

She could hardly think for the blood rushing to her head. "I might indeed like to try a few others." She ground her hips in a rotating motion, astounded that the position could create such different sensations. "Does this particular position have a name?"

"Well, it is translated from Sanskrit, you understand." She felt him lift his buttocks a little, his cock thrusting deeper as he did so, until she felt as if it were about to reach her womb. "And the translation is not as poetic as it could be. But in English it is called Reciprocal Sight of Posteriors." To reinforce the name he caressed her buttocks.

She giggled. Anything less poetic she could not imagine. Still, she had no quibbles with the position itself.

"Touch yourself as you sit on me. Tease your clit with your fingers while I fuck you."

Her hands were free in this position, she realized. She moved them to her nub as he ordered and began to stroke herself in time with his thrusts.

Then, to her delight, she found she could touch and cup his balls, squeezing and caressing them as she sank up and down on his shaft.

With one hand on her nub and the other on his balls, she moved her hips up and down and side to side so every inch of her pussy was loved.

He thrust into her hard and strong, his cock angled just perfectly to reach that special place deep in her pussy, the place that made her cry out in pleasure when he reached it.

Leaning all the way forward, she grasped his ankles and changed to a faster up and down movement. To her satisfaction, she heard a strangled cry from Dominic as he sought to control his own pleasure. "Not yet."

He placed his hands on her buttocks to slow her movements. With his hands gripping her ass she lifted up until she felt just the tip of his cock at the entrance to her cunt.

She held there, imagining what his view must be like—his cock slick with her juices only just spreading her pussy lips, her ass once more wide open to his gaze.

She wanted him to touch her there again. She'd enjoyed that most private of caresses a few moments ago, and sought to encourage him, but was uncertain how to put her request. "Touch me as you touched me before," she finally said, shyly.

She felt a finger lightly touch her ass, feather strokes that both tickled and brought unexpectedly exquisite pleasure.

"Like this?"

Unable to speak, she simply held there, hips moving ever so slightly, signaling her desire to have him continue. After a few moments of caressing, he took hold of her hips and pulled her close to him, burying his cock once more deeply inside her.

The surprise of the fullness of him all the way inside tipped her over the edge. He kept himself there as her climax overwhelmed all her senses, holding himself still so she could milk every last drop of pleasure from the feeling of his shaft deep inside her.

Finally the throbbing of her orgasm subsided. She wanted nothing more than to sink down onto the floor of the carriage and sleep off her satisfaction and her lassitude, but he was not yet finished. His cock, still hard as a wooden post, twitched with need deep in her pussy. "I have one more position I want to show you. Stand up for a moment."

Doing as she was bid, she stood up and stretched in the sunlit carriage, knowing he was looking at her with pure lust. She turned in a full circle, then faced him as he stood up, too, his erection hard and jutting from his firm, smooth stomach.

He pulled her over to the window, where a couch was conveniently placed, the lace curtains barely shading the view of the green countryside flowing past. "Kneel on the couch," he instructed her, standing behind her, his cock nestled firmly in between her buttocks.

She knelt, and steadied herself from the rocking of the train by grabbing the backrest. Her breasts spilled out over the backrest, pressing against the glass of the window. If they were to pass a village now, everyone would see her naked in the carriage. They would see Dominic, naked behind her. They would know that she was kneeling on the couch in the carriage being fucked from behind. The thought did not bother her, indeed it felt so gloriously wicked to know that anyone could see her like this, and yet she was safe from their sidelong glances and nasty whispers. They would never know who she was, and she would never see them again. To the people who caught a glimpse of her bare breasts, she would forever be the unknown naked woman on the train. No one would ever know her as Caroline Clemens.

Dominic's hands were on her buttocks, and she sensed him kneel to look once more at her cunt.

He breathed lightly on her very wet opening, touching it lightly with his fingers, spreading her open for his view. "What a joy to behold women are. So pretty, so much like a flower." He admired her for a few moments more before standing up and without warning rapidly thrusting his cock all the way into her.

Her breasts pressed against the window and her fingers gripped the backrest of the couch.

This time there was no hesitation in his movements as he relentlessly took her from behind. Farmsteads and barns appeared in view and disappeared again as the train traveled on, while each time he plunged into her it brought a cry to her lips and drew her one step closer to another orgasm.

His pace quickened and his grip on her buttocks grew more powerful until suddenly he pushed harder than ever into her. He held her still while his body quivered as the tremors of his orgasm washed over him with a roar.

She felt his hot seed pumping into her, and the knowledge that he was spending deep inside her tipped her over the edge. The world outside diminished to a pinpoint, and she cried out once more in an abandonment of delight.

"My God, Caroline, if that had been any better, I would be a dead man." He collapsed over her, his cock slowly losing its hardness inside her. "I don't know how much longer I will survive having you around."

His words put a chill into her soul. She had not thought she could delight him so much that the pleasure got too much for him. Was he already thinking of letting her go? "Am I too much for you?" How long did most men keep a mistress? She did not know for sure, but surely it would be longer than a month or two. Especially given the price that Dominic had paid to enjoy her company. He would

surely want her a year or more, just to recoup his investment.

"You would be too much for half a dozen men, but I would
not give you a chance to prove it. You are mine, and mine you
will stay."

The racing of her heartbeat steadied. He was not tired of
her. Not yet. His idle words were nothing but that—they
meant nothing. "Even if it kills you?" she teased.

"Then I will die a happy man," he said as he eased his
weight off her.

She collapsed onto the couch, no longer mindful of her nakedness. Too satisfied to move, she watched his fine muscles
as he walked over to a cupboard where he selected a warm
blanket and returned to the couch.

Lying down next to her, he covered them both and nuzzled
close, breathing in her scent. "You are mine, Caroline," he
murmured sleepily as he hugged her to his chest. "I will not
let you go. Not ever."

Lying there in his arms, she hugged her own to her chest.
He did not mean anything deep or lasting by his words, she
was sure of it. She belonged to him for now, and that was all
that mattered to him.

The present was all that mattered to her as well. The future would have to take care of itself—she had no breath to
waste worrying about it. It would come soon enough.

And in the meantime she would strive to be sensible,
as sensible and hardheaded as any gay girl who walked the

streets to earn her supper. She was one of them now, and she must remember her position in life. It was sheer foolishness to let the flower of hope blossom in her chest that maybe, one day, Dominic would come to care for her, maybe even to love her.

He would never love her. How could he, when she did not—when she could not—love him in return? Simply put, she could not afford to. He would leave her eventually, when he found a woman who enticed him more than she did, or when he fell in love and decided to marry.

He would never fall in love with her. Men did not fall in love with courtesans. Courtesans were for fucking. Wives were for loving.

She was a warm body for Dominic to sink his shaft into whenever he felt like coming—nothing more than that. Men did not need to have softer feelings for a woman to enjoy fucking her.

Nonetheless she was cozy under the blanket next to him for now, as the train rattled on.

She looked at him uncertainly, wondering what he was thinking, but he had already fallen asleep under the warm blanket, a peaceful boyish look on his face.

By the time she woke again, they were nearly at their destination. Her dress had dried while they both dozed, but the front was marred with an ugly stain. Caroline clambered back into it with a moue of distaste, feeling horribly disheveled. It was hardly the way to make a good first impression on arrival.

Dominic stayed her with a hand on her arm when she moved toward the door of the railway carriage. "I have not been exactly forthcoming with you as to our destination," he murmured.

She looked at him, puzzled. What did he consider so unforthcoming about telling her they would be staying at a house in Cornwall by the sea? What else did she need to know?

"We shall be staying in a rather unusual house, I fear," he said, as if reading her mind. "A house for the entertainment of married couples."

His words rang uncomfortably in her head. "Are you taking me to a bawdy house?" she asked slowly. It was his right to take her where he pleased, she supposed, and she knew she was his whore, but she did not like it. Not at all. Though she was his mistress, she still deserved to be treated with some respect.

"No, not that. But it is a place where we can explore our sensuality in the company of other like-minded couples."

A sudden suspicion flashed across her mind. "Have you been there before?" she asked as casually as she could manage. "With other women?" Not that it was her place to care—she simply wanted to know.

"No, this is all as new to me as it is to you. My friend who lent me the railway carriage told me about the place. He highly recommended it. In fact, he will be there with his wife at the same time as we will be. Mrs. Hughes is a very fashionable woman. I hope you will like her."

Caroline groaned to herself. Dominic did not know English society very well or he would never even think of introducing her to the wife of one of his friends. She was nothing more than a whore. Mrs. Hughes would not deign to talk to her, she would despise her.

So much for her hopes of a peaceful holiday in Dominic's company without the strictures of rest of the world to worry about.

Dominic did not seem to notice her uneasy silence during the carriage ride to the house where they would be staying. It soon came into view, an imposing manor house set in the middle of some glorious gardens. If nothing else, she would at least enjoy exploring those.

To her relief, their hostess immediately noticed the state of Caroline's gown, and without saying a word about it, detached her from Dominic's side and led her to her room, where she could change.

A half hour later, freshly washed and in a clean new gown, Caroline left the bedroom with some trepidation to rejoin Dominic. Much as she would have preferred to, she could not hide out alone in her room all week.

The room she had left him in was empty, but the French doors that led outside to a pretty paved courtyard were open.

The fine weather and the beauty of the garden tempted her outside.

Not until she was outside did she see the woman reclining on the wooden bench, her eyes closed and an expression of utter peace on her face.

She tiptoed past, not wanting to wake her, but as she passed, the other woman's eyes opened and she sat up with a cry of delight. "Hello. You must be one of the new guests who arrived today. Come, sit down and say hello. I'm Cora, Cora Hughes. My husband and I have been here for most of a week already. We visit here as often as we can."

Caroline felt a flush of red creep over her face. In all fairness, she could not force her acquaintance on an unsuspecting woman. "I don't think you would want to make my acquaintance," she said, her voice brittle. At that moment she almost hated Dominic for putting her in such an awkward position.

"Why ever not?"

"My father was a bankrupt," she stated baldly. "I came here with Mr. Savage. I am not ... we are not ... Mr. Savage is not my husband." Truly, she did not feel shame for herself, but she hated having to explain her position. What would women such as Mrs. Hughes know about poverty and desperation and the lengths to which they could drive a woman? It would not take much for her to hate Mrs. Hughes, too, with her easy manners and her air of wealth and privilege. Mrs. Hughes would never have known what it was like to feel crippling hunger pangs, or the agony of seeing her family waste away to nothing in front of her.

Mrs. Hughes waved one hand airily. "Oh, who cares about little things like that anymore—such straitlaced morality is terribly outdated nowadays. I certainly don't care about such trifles. Besides, you might not want to talk to me if the thought of scandal bothers you. Gareth and I created a huge to-do last year but nobody except for a couple of malicious old biddies even remembers it now, let alone cares a fig about such an old piece of gossip."

Caroline's mouth fell open in shock, her hatred evaporating to nothing. "You truly do not mind that I am a ... a gay girl? When you are respectably wed?" Truly, Mrs. Hughes was nothing like she had expected. "Will your husband not object to you keeping company with me?"

Mrs. Hughes patted the bench next to her in an invitation to sit down. "What gives me the right to cast stones at you? I am hardly guiltless myself in that regard. And Gareth knows better than to try and choose my friends for me. Now, come sit down and introduce yourself properly."

Too surprised to do anything but obey, she dipped into a light curtsey. "I am Caroline." She sat down on the bench as far away as she could from Mrs. Hughes, still not convinced of her welcome. "Caroline Clemens."

"You are Dominic's friend, I think you said?"

"I am."

Mrs. Hughes reached out and stroked her hair, making Caroline feel like a child to be comforted or a skittish horse to be gentled. "You're quite the beauty. A real unspoiled English rose type. He's a lucky man to have found you."

A genuine warmth flowed from Mrs. Hughes, a warmth that melted away all Caroline's embarrassment and discomfort. "The luck was all on my side. He rescued me from ... from a rather unpleasant situation." She did not see the need to expound on her miserable days in the workhouse, or to explain just how desperate she had been before he took her under his wing.

"And you became his mistress in exchange?"

She nodded.

"I thought as much."

"It was my choice," Caroline said hastily, not wanting Mrs. Hughes to get the wrong idea about the sort of man Dominic was. "He did not pressure me for anything. I could have become a governess or a nursery maid if I had wanted, and he would have helped me find a position. I chose the life I am living of my own free will. And I do not regret it."

"You do not have to justify yourself to me. I am the last person who has the right to judge anyone else. But come, it doesn't do to dwell on the unpleasant things in life. Not when you have arrived here at Sugar and Spice and are ready to enjoy all the delights on offer here." There was a mischievous twinkle in Mrs. Hughes's eye as she spoke. "Would you like me to tell you more about them?"

★ ★ ★

Buoyed by the unexpected hand of friendship that Mrs. Hughes held out to her, Caroline faced the prospect of dinner that evening with reasonable equanimity. The activities at the house, Mrs. Hughes had assured her, were all absolutely voluntary. No one was ever asked to participate in something that made them feel uncomfortable, and they were all free to leave at any time.

Of course, Mrs. Hughes had confided to her with a throaty giggle, it would be a real pity if Caroline and Dominic did not want to join in the fun. Her visits to Sugar and Spice were the highlight of her year. Nowhere else did she fell so free to explore the boundaries of her sensuality and to learn the particular likes of her husband. Her visits here, she assured Caroline, had done more than anything else to teach her how to keep Mr. Hughes her willing slave.

Those words had convinced Caroline to stay and partake, if she could, of whatever games were played at the house. She would be willing to do pretty much anything within reason if she could learn just a few tricks to keep Dominic interested in her, learn how to please him just that little bit better, and find out what enticed him and drew him in and what left him cold.

Her inexperience with men would not keep him interested for long, and would be no great draw card for any other protector now that her virginity was gone. Experience in pleasing men was what she needed now, and where better to learn it from than from the mistress of such a house as this? And from the other guests as well, if they would teach her. Maybe she would approach Mrs. Hughes on the subject later in the week if she got a chance, and ask her to share some of her secrets. She looked over at Dominic as he drew a clean shirt over his naked torso and buttoned it up. She would like him to be her willing slave...

But meanwhile it was high time for her to get dressed herself. Dominic had outfitted her with a number of handsome dinner dresses, and she selected one of her favorites, in a deep creamy yellow. She would have preferred a gray or a mauve, to show proper respect for her father, but she had not liked to ask Dominic to buy her mourning clothes. She was his mistress, after all, and her job was to keep him satisfied. Mourning the death of her parent was her private sphere, only to be indulged in when he was not around to be disturbed at the sight of her tears.

So, for Dominic, she put on the yellow gown, and inwardly begged her father's pardon for her seeming levity.

The parlor where they gathered before dinner was crowded with couples. There must have been six or seven of them altogether, all laughing and smiling as if they were the best of friends. Caroline looked around them swiftly, her eyes searching for a familiar face.

None of them were people she knew. She breathed a sigh of relief. Nobody knew her here. She could remain anonymous. As long as she kept her situation to herself, she would not have to suffer any sidelong glances or nasty comments about her parentage or her lack of morals.

In the middle of the largest group stood Mrs. Hughes, surrounded by laughing couples. Mrs. Hughes beckoned Dominic and her over and introduced them to the rest of the company without so much as a flicker of embarrassment.

Caroline took heart at her easy manner and the friendly smiles of the other guests. By the time dinner was announced some half hour later, she was feeling enough at ease to stand and listen and observe, if not to take an active part in the conversation.

By the time dinner was over, and she had drunk several glasses of tart white wine with her food, she felt as much at home here as she did in her own parlor.

When Mrs. Bertram rapped on her wineglass with her knife to hush the chatter around the dinner table, Caroline was actually looking forward to the next phase of the evening. Whatever Mrs. Hughes had said, surely it couldn't be as shocking as all that. Her dinner companions were all perfectly respectable people and would be at home in any house in Bloomsbury or even in Belgrave Square. Indeed, she thought to herself with a small giggle, she was the least respectable of all of them.

When a hush had fallen over the table, Mrs. Bertram spoke. "Ladies and gentlemen, it gives me great pleasure to welcome you all to my house. To Sugar and Spice."

There was a smattering of applause around the table and one of the gentlemen lifted his glass. "To Sugar and Spice."

"To Sugar and Spice," Caroline echoed with the rest of the company, lifting her wineglass to her lips once again.

"Now that dinner is over, we have some entertainment planned for the evening. As we have some newcomers here tonight," she nodded graciously at Caroline and Dominic, "I thought it best if we were to start off with a simple game of Shadows."

A game of Shadows? Caroline giggled out loud. She had not played that since she was a small girl, when her mother was still alive. As children, they had rigged up an old white sheet in the schoolroom, then turned out all the gas lamps but one, and taken turns at creeping behind the white sheet to throw a shadow that looked as unlike their natural self as possible. Now she knew that Mrs. Hughes had been exaggerating. There was nothing naughty about a simple, childish game of Shadows.

"The men will be the shadows first," Mrs. Bertram pronounced, getting to her feet. "Come, ladies. Let us go into the parlor while they prepare themselves."

While they were at dinner, the parlor had been transformed with a huge white sheet dividing the room in two. Mrs. Bertram pulled it back with one hand and waved them through to the other side, where a row of chairs was laid out. "Sit down. The men will not be long, I'm sure."

Caroline sat down at the end of the row, next to Mrs. Hughes, grinning at the thought of the forfeit she would demand of Dominic when she guessed him correctly. She was sure she would be able to recognize his gait, however he tried to disguise himself.

Mrs. Bertram extinguished all the lights, leaving only one burning on the other side of the curtain. Caroline watched as her bulky shadow glided out of the door, and another, rather taller and slimmer one, strode in.

At first she did not realize what she was seeing in the shadows. She blinked once, and then again.

No, she was not mistaken. The shadow was of a man wearing a top hat, and nothing else. To make matters worse, when he turned in side profile to the sheet, it was clear that he was sporting a sizable erection, which stood stiffly out from his body, bouncing a little in time with his footsteps.

She gazed at the shadow, fascinated, as he strode back and forth behind the sheet. So this is what Mrs. Hughes had been meaning to warn her about.

The woman on the other side of her was giggling fit to burst. "I know who you are, John," she called out between spurts of laughter. "I would recognize that bend in your cock anywhere."

Caroline looked at the shadow again. He did have a rather peculiar crook in his cock, though it had hardly been noticeable until it was pointed out.

The shadow took off his top hat and bowed low. "You are quite correct, my dear, as always."

His wife giggled in delight at being proved correct. "You have to pay a forfeit."

"You may have my hat." Pulling back the curtain, quite unashamed, he walked into their half of the room and handed his top hat to his wife with a bow. "I will redeem it later."

He had been so close to her that she could see every curl of hair at the base of his proud shaft, every vein that ran along its hard length. If she had reached out her hand, she could have stroked his naked buttocks as he passed her. In fact, she caught sight of the woman seated on the other side of his wife doing so, and neither he nor his wife had complained.

Caroline swallowed. This week was going to be enlightening in more ways than one.

One by one the men of the company made their appearance behind the shadow curtain, each of them wearing no more than a single item of clothing. The sole exception was the man who, as far as she could tell, was wearing both his socks.

One by one their wives guessed them correctly, until there were quite a number of forfeits to be paid.

Eventually Dominic made an appearance as a shadow. Though he wore his shirt and tried to disguise himself by hunching over and walking with a limp, she knew at once that it was him. Besides, he was the last of the company.

At the sight of him, so nearly naked behind the curtain, her heart skipped a beat, as it had failed to do for any of the other men. Back and forth she watched him limp, amused at his attempts to disguise himself. Finally she called out in a loud voice, "I am sure that must be Dominic. See how he creaks and groans with old age. Ah, deary me, what a curse it is to have an ancient husband with no courage in him."

The other women all shrieked with laughter at her words.

Behind the curtain, Dominic straightened up and stomped over to the curtain. "I see you have no respect for my modesty, wench," he said, peering out at her with a mock scowl. "And not much respect for my person, either."

Letting the curtain fall, he pulled off his linen in the shadows. He drew the curtain back just enough to toss the shirt at Caroline's feet. "You may claim a forfeit from me this time, but I shall be sure to claim one back from you later in the evening."

The forfeited clothing was gathered together in a pile by the door, as the men trickled in again. Dominic was the last, entering rather shamefacedly in trousers and jacket but no shirt. A couple of the women made noises of appreciation at the sight of his bare chest. It was a particularly nice chest, she had to concede, smooth and muscled, without a hint of flab. Still, she wished he had his shirt on so none but she could see his naked chest.

Mrs. Hughes's voice came soft and amused in her ear. "You're looking at him as if you want to eat him up. And as if you wanted to claw the eyes out of the other women who are thinking the same."

She shook her head. Yes, she desired him, as she had from the first moment, but her feelings had grown to be more than that. Far more. He was hers, and she wanted to keep him to herself. The sight of other women looking at him with desire made her feel positively sick to her stomach.

She could not put her finger on the moment when her feelings toward Dominic changed, when she had become so possessive of his affection. She had not always felt that way about him. Before today he had been her meal ticket. A perfectly pleasant and agreeable meal ticket, and a generous one, and one to be prized, but a meal ticket all the same.

When had he become not just her savior, but her very heart and soul?

Eight

As soon as the men were all assembled in the sitting room, Mrs. Bertram led the women back through the curtain and into the neighboring room, which they were using as a dressing room.

"You will have worked out the rules of the game by now, I imagine," she said, a smile on her face. "All of you get to choose one item of clothing to wear. All the rest must be discarded. If your husband—or anyone else's husband, for that matter—chooses correctly, then you must pay a forfeit of the item you are wearing. If they do not guess who you are, then there is no forfeit to be paid. Are you ready?"

Caroline crossed her arms over her chest and tried to suppress her shivers. The thought of parading naked, or very nearly so, in front of all the men in the next-door room made her squirm with embarrassment. Would Dominic really want to see her like that, undressed for everyone to gaze on? Would he not think she was a loose woman?

Of course, she *was* a loose woman. That was the irony of it. She simply didn't want to appear like one in front of him.

"Can I give you a piece of advice?" Mrs. Bertram asked the roomful of women. She moved over to a chest and flipped the lid open, revealing a profusion of wigs and clothing and other things whose purpose Caroline didn't even like to guess at. "I have some items here that may help you to confuse the gentlemen. Choose yourself a partner, one who looks most like you, and dress them as you would dress yourself. Show them how to walk like you do and how to stand like you do. None of your husbands will be able to guess you then, I'll warrant."

Mrs. Hughes grabbed Caroline by one of her wrists. "You look the most like me out of all the others here. Come be my partner."

Caroline shook her head. She looked nothing at all like the glamorous Mrs. Hughes. "Surely Mrs. Warren is more like you than I am," she said, naming the second most elegant woman in the room, whose long brown hair matched the length of Mrs. Hughes auburn locks.

Mrs. Hughes shook her head. "Mrs. Warren is too skinny and her breasts are virtually nonexistent. Gareth will never believe that she is me. But you are just a fraction taller than I am, and about the same size and shape. We could pull this off."

"But my hair ..."

"You shall wear a wig to disguise your hair. As shall I. None of them shall know us and we shan't have to pay a forfeit at the end. What a great joke that will be on the men. Come, dress me just as you would attire yourself to go behind the shadow curtain."

Hesitantly, Caroline allowed herself to be pulled into the other woman's enthusiasm. "I could never parade naked, as the men did."

"You are allowed to keep one article of clothing," Mrs. Hughes reminded her. "Just remember that if you are guessed, you must pay the forfeit and give it to your man in the presence of all the rest." She unhooked the buttons of her dress and let it fall to the floor. "I would not mind for myself, but I do not think you would like them leering at you."

Mrs. Hughes had a point. If disguising herself like her new friend would prevent her from having to waltz out naked in front of all the gentlemen, it was worth a try.

Of course, she could always walk away from the evening and refuse to play the game, but that would displease Dominic, and she did not want to do that. He had brought her here knowing what took place in this house, and had played the game himself with a good spirit. She could do no less in her turn. "I would wear my chemise. It would hide my shape more than any other article of clothing. And if I were to be guessed, why then, no one would be able to see later on that I had no chemise on under my dress."

"Your chemise?" Mrs. Hughes pouted. "I am proud of my body and do not care who looks on it. I had thought merely to wear one of my garters."

"My chemise," Caroline replied firmly. "If we are to swap characters, we must do it properly. Dominic would never believe that I would appear behind the shadow curtain wearing nothing but a garter."

Reluctantly Mrs. Hughes stripped down to her chemise, a frothy creation of finest lawn that floated around her as she walked.

Caroline nodded her approval. "It's near enough like mine to pass. Now let me see what I can do with your hair." Mrs. Hughes's auburn hair was darker and straighter than her own wavy red-blond locks, but that could soon be fixed. Rummaging around in the chest, she found a wig that closely approximated her own hair. She placed it on Mrs. Hughes's head. "Now, be still while I pin your own hair underneath."

When she was finished, Mrs. Hughes stood in front of her, looking as like her as if they were sisters.

Caroline looked at her critically, still not entirely satisfied. "I know what the matter is. You are too confident in the way you stand. Too sure of yourself. I do not have your confidence or poise."

Ms. Hughes struck an exaggeratedly shy and awkward pose, all knees and elbows. "Is this better?"

Caroline screwed up her nose. "You look much more like me when you do that." It was a depressing thought. "You'll do."

Mrs. Hughes clapped her hands together. "Excellent. Now it is my turn to dress you as I would dress myself. Off with all your clothes."

"I am allowed to keep on one article of clothing," Caroline reminded her as she unfastened her dress.

"Precisely. But I get to say what that article is."

"My chemise?" Caroline suggested hopefully.

Mrs. Hughes merely laughed. "That would give the game away at once. Gareth would never believe I would wear my chemise when I had a chance to go naked."

Caroline gulped as she removed her chemise. "My pantalettes, then?" Surely Mrs. Hughes would let her keep them.

"Certainly not. Take them off, too."

"But I am wearing nothing else."

"Nonsense. You still have two stockings, two slippers, two garters, two gloves, and a pretty hat. Maybe I will let you keep the hat."

"I will look utterly ridiculous," Caroline grumbled, conveniently forgetting how taken she had been by the sight of the naked man wearing only his hat. "Stark naked with a hat perched on top of my head."

"If we are to swap characters, we must do it properly," Mrs. Hughes said, parroting her earlier words back at her. "On second thought, take off the hat. It will be easier to fix a wig on you if your head is bare. I will let you keep a garter instead."

"You want me to go behind the curtain and show myself to the company wearing nothing but a garter?" Caroline shook her head. This game was going too far. She no longer wanted to play, not even to make Dominic happy with her. "I shall be too ashamed."

Mrs. Hughes laughed at her modesty. "You forget, everyone will think you are me. Come, pull off your stockings and let me arrange your hair."

Caroline backed away, on the verge of turning tail and running from the room, from the house itself. "I cannot do this." Maybe it was not too late to become a governess after all. In Ireland, or somewhere equally far away where her fall from grace could be concealed.

"You want to capture Dominic's attention, don't you?" Mrs. Hughes asked.

Caroline nodded. "He is my security, the only way I have of holding my family together."

"And you want to make him think you are the most desirable woman in the world?"

She would hate it if he were to find her lacking in any way. "I do."

"Then what better way to do it than have every man in the room looking at you, wanting you, wishing they were in his place? If he sees you have other options, that you stay with him from choice rather than from necessity, he will prize you all the more, and work hard to keep you happy. You want him to keep you, don't you?"

Caroline nodded slowly, giving in to the inevitable. She liked Dominic and desired him, and he was kind to her. She did not want to have to find another protector—she wanted Dominic to keep her.

In the chest, they found a wig of long dark hair, close enough to Mrs. Hughes's length to pass muster. It made the top of Caroline's head itch dreadfully, but she gritted her teeth and bore it as best she could. Though she would go through with this game, she was still less than happy about it. But then, she would have suffered a good deal more than a scratchy wig to have her true identity disguised.

"Now strike a pose for me," Mrs. Hughes declared.

Caroline struck a pose, hiding as much as she could of her naked body behind the thick hair of the wig.

Mrs. Hughes pushed the hair away from Caroline's breasts, her fingers lingering on the soft curves. "Be proud of your body as I am of mine. Do not try to hide it. You have such a beautiful shape, it should not be hidden under all that hair."

Even in the company of her sisters, Caroline had never been comfortable with her nakedness. She blushed under Mrs. Hughes's open scrutiny. "I shall try to act as confidently as you would."

"That would be wisely done of you," the other woman replied wryly. "For if you are anything less than confident, you will be found out right away."

They had taken some time in getting ready, and the men were clearly getting impatient. Cries of encouragement and shouts for them to hurry along and show themselves were getting louder by the minute.

As Caroline practiced walking with confidence, and Mrs. Hughes covered herself with her hair and attempted a modest look, Mrs. Bertram sent the first woman off to pose behind the curtain.

Howls of delight and appreciative catcalls greeted her entrance. "That's my wife," one of the men called out, loud enough for all of them in the next room to hear. "I'd know her shape anywhere."

One of the women clapped her hands quietly together with barely suppressed glee. "That's William speaking," she said in a whisper. "With such confidence, too. He thinks Mrs. Kingsley is me, just as Mrs. Bertram said he would. I shall never let him forget this. Never. It will be worth at least that lovely ruby bracelet I saw the other week in Harrods."

There were cries of disbelief when Mrs. Bertram pronounced the men wrong in their guess and sent another woman behind the curtain to test their mettle.

One by one the women posed behind the curtain as someone else, and one by one the men guessed their identity wrongly, until only Caroline and Mrs. Hughes were left.

Caroline looked beseechingly at Mrs. Hughes. Now that the time was very near, the butterflies in her stomach were turning cartwheels and she thought she might be sick. "You go out first," she whispered. "Please. I'm not ready yet."

Mrs. Hughes shot her a grin as she minced to the door. "I will be as modest as a dewdrop and convince them all that I am you."

By now the men had gotten wind that something fishy was up and were no longer calling out the names of their wives with such confidence. When Mrs. Hughes walked through to stand behind the shadow curtain, only a few appreciative whistles disturbed the mutterings.

Caroline, a shawl thrown over her shoulders to keep the chill off her naked body, listened to them with growing unease. They didn't like being made to look like fools. The guessing game had gotten serious. She should have conquered her fears and gone first.

Joining the group of women by the door, she strained her ears to listen.

"I would have sworn it was Caroline," she heard Dominic say, "if it hadn't been that every other guess we've made this evening has been wrong, and every man was sure of himself. Besides, now that I think about it, there is something not quite right about her. Nothing that I can put my finger on, but I do not think it is her."

"One thing I'm sure about is that it is not Cora," Mr. Hughes said. "I cannot imagine my dear wife wearing a shift if she had the chance to go naked. She is proud of her body, and rightly so. And her hair is longer than that woman's."

"Maybe that is where we have been going wrong," Dominic suggested. "Maybe we should guess the person we think is the least likely, instead of the most."

"We haven't been doing very well so far," grumbled one of the other men. "May as well take a chance and say this is Mrs. Hughes and be done with it."

"What the devil." Mr. Hughes gave a loud laugh. "If we're

going to be wrong, we may as well be properly wrong and be done with it. Cora, I guess that it is you behind the curtain."

There was the scraping noise of the curtain being drawn back and then a moment of stunned silence before the room erupted in a roar of triumph. "We got her. By Jove, we got her."

"Congratulations, husband. You guessed me correctly. Now come and claim your forfeit." There was a rustle of clothing. In her mind's eye Caroline could picture Mrs. Hughes raising her arms and pulling off her chemise to reveal her nakedness to the company. All the men would be staring at her, admiring her body, gazing at her firm, white breasts and rounded buttocks, and at the thatch of red hair that lay between her legs.

All the men. Even Dominic.

At that thought, she threw off the shawl, ready to take her turn. She would show Dominic that she was as brave as Mrs. Hughes could ever be, and that her body was just as well-rounded and desirable. If she had to prove it with an audience, then so be it. Prove it she would.

Dominic's breath caught in his throat at the sight of the last woman in the company behind the shadow curtain. Braver than the others, she came out seemingly wearing nothing at all. That is, until he caught the glimpse of a garter worn high up on one of her legs. Apart from that one thin scrap of satin and lace, she was utterly naked.

Utterly beautiful, too. Her breasts were made for a man's

hand, and her buttocks shapely and full, begging to be stroked. Or smacked.

The thought of laying his hands on those buttocks made his cock fully hard in his trousers.

As if the sight of Mrs. Hughes's red-haired beauty hadn't been enough to make him ache for release, now it was this little witch's turn. Not that he didn't like Caroline by far the best of the bunch, but he was no monk wedded to chastity. And looking at another man's woman never hurt—so long as he didn't go any further than looking.

He looked around the room, wondering which man had the joy of being married to her.

Nobody was rising up to claim her.

Gareth Hughes, though, was looking remarkably thoughtful. "If I hadn't had Cora in my arms just half a minute ago, I would swear it was her," he said. "She has Cora's hair, her height, her shape, and most of all her delightful lack of clothing. All of it screams Cora. But it can't be her." He held up the chemise that he had pulled off her body. "I have her forfeit here."

A dark suspicion was brooding in Dominic's mind. The last person he would expect to see cavorting so confidently behind the curtain, striking wanton poses with such insouciance, was his Caroline. But hadn't Cora Hughes been attired exactly the opposite to what Gareth had expected?

He stood up and gestured at the others. "Ordinarily I would never believe she would be my Caroline," he began. "The hair is too long, for a start. But we have all seen on Mrs. Hughes what a difference a wig can make."

"Damn near played me for a fool," Gareth Hughes growled.

"I don't think she is Caroline. I really don't. She looks nothing like her, moves nothing like her. And I cannot imagine Caroline parading behind a curtain wearing nothing but a garter." He paused for a moment. "Which is why I am so sure it *is* her. If you are Caroline, come out and show yourself. You owe me a forfeit."

Caroline heard Dominic's words with a sinking feeling in her breast. Their elaborate disguise had been all for nothing. He had found her out.

Shyly she poked her head around the curtain. "You shall have your forfeit," she said, fumbling with the garter around her leg.

A growl of disappointment went around the gentlemen. "Not so fast," Dominic said. "Come on out where we can all see you."

Caroline lifted her head high and stepped out from behind the curtain, her arms at her sides, feeling truly like a courtesan, a beautiful and desirable courtesan, for the first time. If Dominic wanted to show her off before the company, then she would show herself proudly. She would not stoop to vainly trying to hide as much of herself as she could behind her hands.

Dominic beckoned her over to stand in front of him.

She could feel the eyes of the men in the room on her as she walked obediently over and stood before him, nose-to-nose. The knowledge that every man's gaze was firmly on her burned away her shyness. They wanted her. At that moment all of them wanted her. They would be hard in their trousers with the sight of her and they all ached to own her, to possess her.

With a growing sense of power, she could feel the waves of lust rolling off them as she displayed herself to them all. Their desire for her stoked her own lust. Though it was warm in the room, her nipples were peaked into hard buds that longed to be fondled. In between her thighs she could feel the telltale wetness begin to seep out of her pussy at the thought of all the cocks in that room, hard as stone for her.

"You tried to make a fool out of all of us." Dominic's words were harsh, but the tone of his voice was like a lover's caress. "All of you women did."

"You can't make a silk purse out of a sow's ear," she retorted. "We merely decided to work with what we had."

His glare turned into an outright scowl. "Give me my forfeit, woman."

She pushed him back into his chair and placed her foot on his knee. "Take it for yourself."

He gave a hiss of indrawn breath as he looked at her standing in front of him, her pussy wide open, its wetness plainly visible. His fingers trembled as he pulled the pale blue garter down her thigh and over her foot. "Are you trying to kill me, Caroline?" he murmured as he blindly took his prize. His eyes seemed to be glued in place, looking at her, open in invitation. "I want to fuck you so damn badly I'm about to disgrace myself in the middle of the company and come in my trousers just from looking at your wet pussy."

She drew one finger through her nest of curls, wetting it with her juice, and then placed it on his lips as he gazed at her, completely stunned. "Later, Dominic, later," she promised in a sultry voice. Then she took her foot off his knee and gave him a saucy wink before she sauntered off again. If she was to act like Mrs. Hughes, she might as well carry it off until the bitter end.

Dominic sat immobile for a moment, the taste of Caroline on his lips. He would never have dreamed it possible that she would act like such a wanton, that she would show off her nakedness with such aplomb, and then touch herself openly while others watched her every movement.

By God, he was a lucky man. She was more desirable than any other woman here, and more packed with guile than a basketful of snakes.

He owed her a punishment for her trickery in trying to pretend she was Cora Hughes. She had given him a forfeit, and he would make her pay to regain her garter.

He smiled to himself. Oh, yes, he would make her pay.

★ ★ ★

The other women had already dressed themselves. Caroline threw on her pantalettes and chemise as quickly as she could and hurriedly fastened her gown over the top. By the look in Dominic's eyes when she left him moments ago, she was due some retribution for the trick she had played on him.

Not that she and Cora were solely responsible for the men's failure to guess their identities, but they were the only two who had been found out and had to pay a forfeit. The ire of the whole group would be taken out on them.

As soon as she had buckled her slippers back on her feet, Mrs. Hughes took her arm and the pair of them entered the room, trailing behind the others. The curtain had been removed and the men stood on one side, their faces as grim as avenging angels.

Mrs. Bertram was seated by the basket of forfeits. "Welcome back, ladies. And may I congratulate you all on your superb performances. You nearly tricked them all."

"We got two of them," Mr. Hughes growled. "And now we are going to make those two pay, even though we can't touch the rest of them."

Dominic stepped forward. "Caroline first, as she was the last to be guessed."

Mrs. Bertram nodded her agreement and picked Caroline's garter out of the pile. "Here is a thing, and a very pretty thing," she called. "What shall be done by the owner of this very pretty thing?" She looked around the room at the gentlemen gathered there. "What say you, Mr. Savage, who found her out? What price will you demand for the return of this pretty garter?"

There was a quick conference among the men and then Dominic spoke. "It is agreed that she shall choose one of three signs." The wicked light in his eye did not bode well.

Nervously, Caroline stood in front of Mrs. Bertram and allowed a scarf to be bound over her eyes.

Dominic stood behind her. "This is the first sign," he called out.

Caroline could not see or sense what motion he was making—a kiss, a pinch, or a box on the ear. Whatever she chose was what she would receive from all the company.

"The second sign."

A ripple of laughter went around the room, but Caroline could see nothing. She waited in darkness until he spoke again. "This is the third sign."

The ripple of laughter expanded into a wave, spilling out every corner of the room.

She licked her lips. "I choose sign number one."

She pulled the blindfold off her eyes and wheeled around to face Mrs. Bertram. "I do not trust Mr. Savage to tell me the truth. What was the first sign? What forfeit must I pay?"

Mrs. Bertram shook her head sorrowfully. "I'm afraid the first sign was that for a spanking."

Dominic took her hand and pulled her over to a sofa. "And a well-deserved spanking it will be."

"You men are simply poor losers," she protested. Though she had chosen what was likely the worst sign of the three, she wasn't in the least bit afraid of paying the forfeit. Gentlemen never smacked a lady. The worst she could expect would be a light rap on her knuckles.

Her confidence turned to dismay when Dominic upended her over his knee and flipped her skirts above her waist. "Put me down," she squealed, trying in vain to pull her skirts down over her pantalettes again. "This is not funny." She had exposed herself all she was going to for one day.

Dominic had other ideas. "A spanking on your bare bum is what you deserve," he said, holding her effortlessly across his knee. "And it's what you're going to get. Will someone volunteer to hold this wildcat down while I take down her pantalettes?" He said this last to the men, who were standing around watching his struggle with smirks on their faces.

A couple of the men stepped forward. "I guess since I can't punish my wife for her tricks, I will have to make do with yours instead," one of them said, grabbing hold of her legs in an iron grip before she could kick him away.

"Exactly my sentiments," the other replied, pinning down her arms so she could not move.

"Thank you, gentlemen." Dominic's hands snaked around her front toward the fastening of her pantalettes, pulling on the ribbons that tied them together.

This was not the sort of forfeit she had expected to have to pay. Dominic would not get away with this as easily as he'd counted on. She tried to wriggle and squirm out of their grip but couldn't break free.

She shivered as her pantalettes were slowly pulled down her immobile legs, exposing her bottom to the whole room.

"What a fine rump for a spanking." Having dismissed his helpers with his thanks, Dominic held her down with one hand and caressed her bare bottom with the other. "I suppose I must be polite and invite you ladies to go first."

One after the other the ladies lined up to spank her, giving her baby taps with the tips of their fingers, taps that would not have hurt a sparrow.

"Now that that farce of a forfeit is out of the way," Dominic said, his voice dripping with disgust, "let the real spanking begin. Men, spank her as you think she deserves."

The first slap on her bare bottom made her flesh burn hot and caused her to squeal in indignation. "Ow, that hurt." Forfeits were not supposed to be painful. Embarrassing, maybe, but never more than that.

Her punisher gave a satisfied cackle. "Good. It was meant to." He followed up his first blow with half a dozen more, all of them equally as hard as the first. "That will serve you for playing tricks on us."

As the blows rained down on her bottom, her squirms grew wilder and more frantic, but she could not escape. Dominic held her too tightly for that.

By the time all the men but Dominic had rained spanks down on her, her bottom was stinging, but not in any painful way. To her dismay, the spanking had excited her. By the time they had finished with her, her squirming was more for show than from any desire to escape her punishment.

"What do you think, Caroline?" Dominic ran one hand over her beaten rump and nudged it between her legs to caress her there. "Have you been punished enough?"

"More than enough," she panted, renewing her struggles to rise. If he touched her like that, she would compound her embarrassment one hundred fold by coming as she lay over his knee.

"Are you sure you don't want just a little more?" With one hand he stroked her pussy while with the other he smacked her lightly on her rump.

"Dominic, please." She didn't know whether she was begging for him to stop or to keep going with his torture.

"You're so wet," he whispered. "I think you enjoyed your punishment. I think you enjoyed having all those men smack you on the backside, one after the other."

By now she was beyond answering him coherently. All her thoughts were focused on her pussy, on the mindless delight that was coming nearer with every stroke of his fingers.

"I think you are excited by being smacked and caressed. I think you're about to come, right here, right now." As he spoke, he thrust two of his fingers right into her.

Despite her embarrassment, she couldn't hold back any longer. She arched her back and gave a guttural cry as her orgasm swept over her, before collapsing, boneless, back onto Dominic's lap.

He withdrew his dripping fingers and gave her backside one last caress. "The forfeit is paid," he said, pulling up her pantalettes and flipping her skirts back over her backside. "Caroline has been duly punished."

Gareth chuckled with anticipation. "That makes it Cora's turn to choose the sign. Come, Mrs. Hughes, and on with the blindfold. Time to redeem your forfeit."

Caroline watched as Cora tied the blindfold over her face. Mr. Hughes stood behind her and made the signs that Cora would have to choose between. The first sign was a kiss, nothing peculiar in that. For the second sign he opened his mouth, stuck his tongue out and made as if he were licking something. The third sign was a thrusting motion with his fingers.

Caroline gasped as the import of the signs he was making hit home. Being spanked in public was shameful enough, but what Mr. Hughes was suggesting seemed far worse. Was he really offering Mrs. Hughes up to be touched so intimately as easily as that? And would she not run from such a prospect?

"I choose the second sign," Cora announced.

A murmur of excitement ran through the room. Mr. Hughes just grinned at her and said nothing.

"Well, tell me what I have chosen," she demanded.

"You have chosen a kiss," he replied.

To Caroline's surprise, Cora's face fell slightly. "Just a kiss?" she asked.

"In a very particular place," he amended. "You have chosen to have your pretty pussy kissed by everyone in the room. Make yourself ready to pay your forfeit."

Without hesitation, Cora removed her pantalettes and arrayed herself on the sofa, her arms flung back over her head, her skirts around her waist and her legs wide open. "Come kiss me," she said, her voice full of anticipation. "I'm ready to pay."

Caroline's heart skipped a beat. Were all of them supposed to lick Cora's pussy? The women as well as the men? She had never heard of such a thing.

Her unspoken question was soon answered as one of the women knelt between Cora's legs and applied her tongue industriously to Cora's nub as Cora moaned in pleasure and thrust her hips forward in encouragement.

Courtesan or not, this was definitely more than she could handle. She turned to Dominic, her hand grasping his tightly. The heat of the gas lighting in the room was making her light-headed. "I have paid my forfeit," she whispered. "Can we retire now?" She could not bear to have Dominic help Cora pay her forfeit. The thought of watching him lick another woman in such an intimate way right in front of her made her feel vaguely queasy. He was *her* protector, *her* lover. Mr. Hughes must have been very confident in his wife's love to allow other men to take such liberties with her. But she was not nearly so confident in Dominic's affections to want any other woman to come near him, let alone to touch him in any personal way.

She would rather scratch their eyes out than let anyone else touch him.

Dominic grinned down at her, seemingly amused by her jealous discomfiture. "I have not yet paid mine."

She did not even want to think about what sort of forfeit would be demanded from the men. Dominic was still hers, and while he belonged to her, no other woman was welcome to touch him. If they slipped away quietly, nobody would ever notice they were gone. "Come, you can pay it to me in private."

Nine

Dominic clasped Caroline tightly against him as they walked through the dark corridors back to their room. "You did not enjoy the games?" Maybe he had made a mistake in bringing her here. She was gently bred, after all, and had been a virgin until recently. He should have known it would all be too much for her when Mr. Hughes had warned him that the games they played at Sugar and Spice were not for the faint of heart.

Her slippered feet scuffled quietly along the floorboards as they walked. "I had not expected the shadow game to be so . . ." Her voice trailed off into nothing.

"So amusing? Entertaining? Shocking?"

At each word he suggested, she shook her head. "So powerful," she confessed in a rush. "Before the game started, my knees were like jelly, shaking with terror. If it were not for my fear of disappointing you, I could not have done it. But then, when I came out from behind the curtain and saw everyone staring at my naked body, I felt like a courtesan must feel when she has kings and princes suing for her favors. I felt strong, powerful, as if I had the world at my feet."

A disquieting sensation swept over him at her words. "You liked being the center of attention?"

"I am a courtesan," she said simply. "And tonight I realized for the first time that being a courtesan carries with it a power over men, an ability to make them do your biding, to have them as slaves at your feet."

"Is having one man at your feet not enough for you?" he asked as he opened the door to their bedchamber and ushered her inside. He deliberately kept his tone light, but it was not an idle question for all that. Had he woken a sleeping dragon by bringing her here?

"Their desire made me feel powerful. And I liked to feel such a power."

Her words struck him dumb. He had thought to introduce Caroline to some new games to play with him, to keep them both entertained and thoroughly satisfied and excited about each other. He had not expected that she would find another side of herself, one in which she gloried in her role as seducer of men.

Whatever she might say, Caroline was no courtesan. She was his mistress. She belonged to him and to no one else. He did not want her to even look at another man while she was with him. He wanted to be the center of her universe, to be everything to her.

Damn it all—he wanted her to love him.

He was suddenly glad she had pulled him away from the festivities. It was time she thought of him again, not of the other men they had left downstairs. "So, what forfeit shall you demand of me to redeem my shirt?" He was hard as nails just thinking about it. Whatever she asked of him, he would willingly pay.

She looked undecided. "What forfeit do you think they will be demanding downstairs?"

"A similar forfeit to the one that Mrs. Hughes is paying now, I imagine." Gareth had told him privately that the forfeit for being guessed was one well worth paying, given that it usually consisted of having one's cock sucked by each of the ladies in turn until you spent in one of their mouths. He had almost been sorry to be dragged away from the fun.

Almost.

With Caroline all to himself as he had her now, what need did he have of any other woman?

Her mouth turned down into a pout. "You do not deserve such an easy forfeit," she grumbled. "Not when you had all the company spank me. My bottom is still red and sore from their treatment."

"Ah, but you enjoyed the spanking, didn't you?" he reminded her. "You liked wriggling about on my knee as your bottom got red and hot. When the spanking was over it only took the barest touch on your pussy to make you spend."

"You made me spend in the middle of the company." Her

voice was as near to a complaint as he had ever heard it. "I could not help it, though inside I was dying of embarrassment. They must all think me totally shameless, a perfect wanton."

"Then my forfeit shall be to make you spend again, this time in the privacy of our own room," he said, unfastening the buttons of her gown and slipping it off her shoulders to pool at her feet. "Will that make you happy again?" It would certainly make him happy—he was so stiff with wanting her all evening that he ached to take her right away, hard and fast.

Of her own accord, she slipped out of her chemise and kicked off her pantalettes until she stood before him, quite naked. "That sounds like an appropriate forfeit to me." Her words were a challenge to his hot blood.

Hastily he disposed of his own jacket and trousers and pulled her down next to him on the bed. He would have her on her knees and begging him to fuck her before the night was too much older, or his name was not Dominic Savage.

His fingers tangled in her nest of curls and stroked her pussy. She was dripping wet, and she moved demandingly against his hand, wanting more.

He moved over her, unable to resist the temptation to slide his cock into her moist heat.

In he thrust, meeting with no resistance, only a silky, warm welcome.

Tempted though he was to mindlessly pound into her until

they both reached their peak, he resisted the loss of his self-control with every fiber of his being. He owed her a forfeit, and he would redeem it in such a way that she would never forget this night of lovemaking.

She had enjoyed the backdoor play in which they had indulged in the train carriage. Maybe she would enjoy more of that, taking more of him inside her than his finger.

Engorged though he already was, he felt himself grow even bigger at the thought of taking her in such an intimate fashion.

She gave a whimper of protest when he pulled out of her, grasping onto his shoulders to bring him nearer to her. "Don't go. You haven't paid your forfeit yet."

Her eyes were half closed with desire as she looked up at him. He reached out and brushed a strand of hair from her face. "Tonight I am going to pay my forfeit in a whole new way."

"A new way?" Her eyes opened a fraction wider. "How?"

"Bring your knees up and I will show you." With those words, he took hold of her legs, bending them at the knees until they were pushed up nearly against her breasts, and propped a pillow under her back.

A trickle of juice dribbled from her open pussy. He gathered it up with his finger and moistened her puckered hole with it. "Tonight," he said, as he inserted one finger gently into her ass, "I am going to fuck you here."

Her whole body shivered as he played with her, inserting

a second finger to join the first. Her eyes were wide and she made no noise of protest. She was ready for him.

His cock was slick with her juices. Slipping out his fingers, he replaced them with his cock, pushing gently into her until the head of his cock was inside her.

She panted, gasping for breath, holding herself still for him.

One hand steadied his cock, helping him to resist the urge to plunge deeply into her, while with his other he reached down and stroked her clit. "Does that feel good?"

"I have never felt anything like this before." Her voice was full of wonderment.

He pushed a tiny way farther into her. "Do you want me to stop?" God, how he hoped she said no. He could hardly bear it if she wanted him to pull out now.

"I like it," she confessed, her body writhing against him and taking him farther inside her. "I am so excited I could like anything you do to me tonight. Anything."

Her muscles were gripping him as firmly as a glove. He withdrew a little way and pushed into her again, reveling in the unaccustomed tightness, the feeling of ownership that it gave him. Wanting her to be as wild as he was, he teased her clit with his fingers, stroking and rubbing her until she was mindless with desire.

"Do you like it when I fuck you like this?" he asked, trying to contain his own excitement as he thrust into her with slow and shallow strokes. "Do you like having me in your ass, while I play with your pussy?"

He got no answer but a cry almost of pain as she convulsed beneath his fingers, her pussy throbbing with her pleasure.

He had paid his forfeit.

His own orgasm was so near he was about to burst. Pulling out of her for the last time, he gave himself a final stroke and his seed splattered in burst after burst of ecstasy over her ass.

Spent, he collapsed beside her and took her in his arms. He had taken her now in every way that a man could take a woman. She belonged to him.

Dominic accepted the cup of tea that Mrs. Bertram offered and put it aside untasted. Heaven knows, he hated drinking the insipid stuff, but he wanted Mrs. Bertram's advice, and accepting her invitation to tea seemed the fastest way to reach his goal. Gareth Hughes had sworn by the efficacy of Mrs. Bertram's advice, though he had also warned him that it might seem unconventional at the time.

Mrs. Bertram sipped her tea, smiling over the rim of the cup at him. "What is on your mind, Mr. Savage? You clearly have not come for the tea."

"What else would it be but a woman?" He shrugged. "Caroline is on my mind. She is always on my mind."

"She is a very attractive woman. Remarkably unspoiled and innocent for a woman in her profession. Added to her looks and grace, it is quite a heady combination. She will go far, that one, if she chooses. Any man would have his head turned by such a one as her."

He did not want to hear that from Mrs. Bertram. Not at all. "Caroline is my mistress. That does not make her a whore."

"She is not a kept woman, then? My apologies, I seemed to recall she had told me—"

"I rescued her from the workhouse and she became my mistress in return," Dominic interrupted. "She has known no other man than me."

"She has reason to be grateful to you, then? She has certainly taken a pleasing part in the entertainments the house has to offer. Remarkably accepting and enthusiastic for a newcomer, I thought, and absolutely made for the sport of love. Some women are, you know."

"Grateful is not enough." He slammed his fist down on the flimsy tea table, causing the cups and saucers to rattle dangerously. "I want her to feel more than gratitude toward me. When she looks at me I want her to see more than a wealthy man who has rescued her, a rich man who shares her bed. I want her to see who I really am. I want her to know me."

"You want her to love you?"

"She is everything that I thought I wanted in a woman. Accommodating, eager to please, obedient. I do not regret making her my mistress, not for a single moment. But I cannot get to the heart and soul of her. Her spirit is too elusive to be captured."

"You want her to love you," Mrs. Bertram repeated—a statement this time rather than a question. "And what will you give her in return? Your heart?"

He wasn't talking about himself, he was talking about Caroline. "I want her to open her thoughts and feelings to me," he said stubbornly.

"She is a courtesan. You will not get through to her as easily as that. Her livelihood depends on her mystery."

He had to restrain himself from overturning the tea table, cups and saucers and all, in his frustration. Clearly Gareth Hughes had grossly overestimated Mrs. Bertram's abilities to assist a man to win a woman's affection. "Is that the only advice you can give me?"

"Not at all. I am merely warning you that there is no magic solution. If you want to win Caroline's heart, you will have to work at it. And you will have to convince her that her love will be safe with you. The position of mistress carries little security with it."

The thought of another man's hands on his Caroline made him growl. "I will never let another man have her."

Mrs. Bertram gave a small smile. "It is not me you have to convince of that, but her. Now, if you want Caroline to open up to you, I suggest you first open up to her. Show her something about your previous life, something that will let her see into your heart and soul. You lived in India, did you not?"

"For most of my life."

"Show her what India meant to you. Show her why you loved the place, how it has made you a different man than all the other men she knows."

He steepled his hands together in thought. It was worth a

try. Maybe Caroline would be entertained by learning more about the place he had spent his boyhood. "The music is what I miss most. The music and the dance—the sensuality of the movements and the very Indian harmonies that one never hears in England. Could you perhaps arrange for such a performance while we are here?"

Her brows knitted together in a frown. "I do not know of any Indian musicians in Cornwall, or good Indian dancers, either. Would you know of any Indian natives in London who might be willing to perform?"

The more he thought about the idea, the more he liked it. "I will telegram my valet immediately," he said, getting to his feet, his mind already running on the upcoming entertainment. "If anyone knows, he will know."

Later that week, when Caroline and Dominic stepped into the large public room used for entertainments, they found it transformed into the likeness of an Indian palace. Delicate silks hung over the walls in casual opulence, while colorful throws of scarlet worked with gold were spread over the sofas, which now hugged the central carpet. Incense and perfumed candles burned on the sideboards, infusing the room with a sweet, spicy scent.

Caroline looked about wide-eyed at the decorations. "Is this what it was like in India?"

"I thought you might like a glimpse of what my life there was like. Not the usual day-to-day business of living, but the culture and beauty of the people. Tonight we are going to be treated to dance and music from southern India."

He led her to a sofa covered in silk woven with pictures of elephants and sat next to her, his arm around her shoulder.

Caroline ran one hand over the material, clearly enjoying the texture of the weave. "I cannot imagine what the dance will be like," she said, her voice full of barely suppressed excitement.

"This style of dance is known as Bharata Natyam, and is one of the oldest dance forms of India. It is famous for its grace, purity, and tenderness, and is also supposed to be spiritually uplifting. I have always thought it one of the most beautiful of the classical Indian dances."

A small table was brought to them laden with treats to eat and glasses of champagne. A few other couples joined them before most of the gaslights were dimmed, leaving only the center of the room illuminated. There was polite applause when an elderly man carrying a string instrument entered the lit part of the room, sat cross-legged on a cushion and started playing.

"That music is unlike anything I have ever heard," Caroline whispered. "The sound is completely different than English music. Is all Indian music like this?"

"Indian music has as many forms as western music, but this music is typical of the Bharata Natyam." As he spoke, he poured her a glass of wine and offered her a plate of dried figs.

She accepted the proffered glass and, taking a fig, nestled

contentedly into his lap. "Tell me about the dance we are about to see."

"The dancer, or *patra*, as they are called in India, will not perform a set pattern as English dancers do, but will tell a story with her body. Every movement she makes is part of this story, even those with her hands and her eyes."

"It sounds complicated."

"It is very beautiful. But this dance is difficult in that it has two faces. It has both graceful, feminine movements and strong, masculine ones. A good *patra* is able to express both equally. Anjali Kinra is reputed to be an accomplished *patra*, of this dance in particular. I hope her performance will please you."

Their discussion was interrupted by the dancer herself gliding out onto the rug that was the stage. A slight young woman, she wore a dress of the deepest purple trimmed with shimmering gold thread. Despite her small stature, she nonetheless had a strong air about her—a graceful power of toned muscle that only a dancer could have. The tips of her fingers were painted red, and about her ankles she wore a string of tiny bells that tinkled softly as she moved to the center of the rug.

The musician finished his warm-up piece and paused as the dancer assumed a starting pose, arms high in a graceful arc with fingers splayed, legs in a solid stance.

With a small flourish, the musician began to play and the dancer moved her body sinuously in time with his playing.

As the dance progressed, Dominic kept one eye on the performance and the other on Caroline. He was pleased to see her totally captivated by the music and dance, champagne forgotten and warming in her hand. "The first parts of the dance were to the Hindu god Ganesh, seeking blessing," he whispered in her ear. "In this center piece the dancer is speaking with her hands and body, telling of love and of her longing for a lover." He had requested this particular dance because of its meaning, hoping she would understand what he was trying to convey to her.

In reply, Caroline simply snuggled closer to him.

The dance progressed to its ending where the lovers, both of whom were played by the dancer, were finally united. The yearning and ecstasy were so clear to him, the emotion she projected so powerful, that his eyes misted over and a lump formed in his throat. It always impressed him deeply when a good dancer was able to play both parts so convincingly and seamlessly.

As he quietly raised a handkerchief to his eyes, Caroline looked up at him, and he saw her eyes had also welled with tears.

Holding her close, he yearned for this moment to last for eternity, with Caroline in his arms and feeling such raw emotion that she could not hide behind her usual veneer of polite obedience.

The dancer's work completed, she held her final pose, an attitude that expressed so well how he felt. He was speechless that she could read her audience so well, to dance to their emotion. Though all the best dancers of Bharata Natyam trained for years at their craft, never before had he witnessed such empathy in a performance.

The music stopped and the audience stood and clapped and cheered. With reluctance he released Caroline as they also stood, expressing their appreciation at the performance.

As he stood, he felt the moment was lost forever. How could he ever make plain to Caroline his feelings to the same depth the dancer had?

He was in love with Caroline. That was the only explanation for the empty feeling he felt inside whenever he made love to her, whenever he sat beside her, so close and yet so far away. For him, their relationship had gone beyond that of a successful businessman and his mistress. Whenever he touched her, he was making love to her.

Her feelings, he knew to his cost, were a good deal less complicated. He paid for the pleasure of loving her, and she allowed him to do so. She was a courtesan, a woman who sold her body for profit. Of all men, he had the least right to complain about it. He, and he alone, had made her what she was.

What a fool he had been not to marry her at once, when she was still so dewy-eyed and grateful to him that she would have given him anything he demanded of her. Why had he demanded only her body? Why had he left her heart in her keeping?

Was it possible to touch her heart anymore? Or had she already encased it so deeply in the ice of disillusionment that no man would be able to thaw it out?

Money would buy her favors. He should know—he already purchased and enjoyed them all. But he didn't want such a meaningless exchange anymore. What was the use of possessing her body if her heart and soul were untouched? Such pleasures were empty imitations of the real thing.

No, he did not think her heart could be bought with mere money. It was too precious for that. He could pay the price of her desire, but what would the price of her love be?

The dance had made it clear to him that he wanted more than sex from Caroline. He wanted to win her heart. Sugar and Spice, though a delightful house to visit, was not the place to think of anything but fucking. Not that he had any problem with thinking only about fucking, but he sensed he would never win Caroline's heart that way. Her obedience, yes, but that was no longer enough for him. He wanted her affection, her devotion even. There was so much more to her than a body to pleasure and to be pleasured by. He needed to touch her more deeply than he had so far, to touch her soul. As Mrs. Bertram had rightly guessed, he wanted her to love him.

He resolved to take her away from Sugar and Spice and show her that he prized more than her enthusiasm in the bedroom. "Come for an excursion with me tomorrow."

Caroline's face brightened at the suggestion. Clearly she was genuinely pleased with his proposal. "Where to?"

He liked to see her smile. "I thought we could go to Torquay. It is a pretty seaside town, and not so far away as to make the journey a chore. We can walk along the pier together arm in arm, looking at the fishing boats. Eat ices in the sun, and a good dinner of fried fish and oysters at a local inn. Do what any courting couple would do."

She shook her head. "It sounds very pleasant, but you have no need to court me. You know that I am yours for as long as you want me."

His wanting her was not in question. He needed her to want him in return, to burn for him as he burned for her, to miss him when he went away and to look forward to his return. "On the contrary, I have every need to."

Ten

Caroline sighed happily as they walked arm in arm along the sand the very next morning. "It's been an age since I have visited the seaside. Papa used to take us to Brighton when I was young, when Mama was alive. After she died, he never cared for seaside holidays anymore. Without Mama, he did not seem to want to do anything."

His arm tightened on hers as he turned to look at her. "What did you like best about Brighton when you were a child?"

A dreamy smile crossed her face. She didn't need to think about the answer for even a single moment. "The Punch and Judy shows." She'd watched them in utter fascination—the grotesque puppets with their jerky movements and colorful clothes, Punch with his hooked nose and truncheon, and Judy in her voluminous nightgown, and Toby the dog. Though they were only puppets, they had seemed so real, so much larger than life. "I loved Punch and Judy." Even the puppet master with his cheerful call of "Roo-ti too-i" had proved an irresistible attraction, one that could beckon her from miles across the sands whenever she heard it.

Dominic grinned to see her enthusiasm for a childish puppet show. "Then we shall find one for you before the day is out."

She hardly heard him, her attention having been caught by the sight of a gentle brown donkey with big sad eyes standing on the sand, a halter around its neck. Letting go of Dominic's arm, she hurried over to stroke its velvety nose.

"Donkey rides just two shillings," the man holding it by a rope attached to the halter called out to her. "You won't find a better price or a sweeter-tempered donkey in all of Devon." He gave the donkey a couple of rough pats on its hindquarters and it shook its ears mournfully back again. "See what a lovely nature she has, ma'am. Call me a liar if she ain't the quietest, most placid creature in all of England. A perfect mount for a lady like yourself."

She shook her head, not wanting to spend two shillings on such a piece of frivolity as riding a donkey. "I just wanted to pat her. She's such a pretty thing."

Dominic nuzzled into her neck. "Don't you want a ride?" he whispered into her ear. "On such a lovely donkey?"

"It's two whole shillings," she said quietly.

"The lady wants a ride," Dominic announced to the donkey's owner. Before Caroline could protest, he stepped forward, picked her up around the waist and lifted her onto the donkey's back, where she sat in an awkward sidesaddle.

He tossed a couple of shillings to the donkey's master, who caught them in the air and tucked them away into his waistcoat pocket. "That's the spirit, sir. Nothing's too good for a lady, now, is it, sir? We just live to make their lives happy, eh?"

Caroline clung to the pommel of the saddle as the donkey started off down the beach, its master leading her by the halter. She'd never been on the back of a donkey before, or a horse, either, for that matter. Though her father had always kept a carriage, the horses were carriage horses and not suitable for a lady's mount. Living in London as they did all year, there had never been any opportunity or any reason for her to learn how to ride.

The donkey's gait was lumpy, her body shifting from side to side as she walked. Gradually Caroline relaxed enough to loosen her death grip on the saddle. Though she felt as if she was perched precariously on the top of a moving mountain, she began to enjoy her ride.

The donkey's owner led her along the sands, though the crowds of people enjoying the sunshine on the beach. The water sparkled a silver blue in the sunlight. White-capped waves broke in the shallows and slithered up onto the sand, turning its pale yellow a deep, wet gold. Seagulls wheeled overhead, cawing in hoarse voices and occasionally diving down to pick up tasty scraps of food discarded by the holiday makers. A brisk breeze blew the ribbons of her bonnet into her eyes, and she let go of her grip on the saddle to brush them away.

Down the beach they plodded before returning to where Dominic waited. "Yer wife's a natural there, sir," the man said as Dominic took her around the waist again and lowered her to the ground. "A regular horsewoman. If she does that regular-like, she'd be able to join the hunt and go leaping over fences after foxes in no time. No time at all."

The egregious flattery made Caroline laugh as she took hold of Dominic's arm once more. "I don't think so. But thank you for the ride."

The donkey's master tipped his hat to her and gave her a saucy wink. "You're welcome, ma'am. Come back another day, do."

A brass band was playing on the pier, the shrill notes of the trumpets carrying through the clear air like the sound of a bell. They wandered over the sand together and went to listen. Dominic bought a couple of ices and they ate them as they walked.

"I feel like a child again," Caroline said, licking up the last drops of her strawberry ice. "On a bank holiday by the seaside. Nothing to do but enjoy myself paddling in the ocean, and nothing to worry about beyond whether I could hide the wet ruin of my stockings from the eagle eye of my mother."

"My fondest memories were of my holidays up in the mountains," Dominic said. "I suppose they were like your seaside in a way." He kicked idly at a stone with the toe of his boot as they walked along. "When the summer sun grew too fierce and the city was like the inside of an oven, my mother would pack us all up and take us to the mountains for a couple of months, until the worst of the heat had passed. It was cooler there."

Caroline's forehead creased into a frown. "I thought all of India was hot."

He gave a bark of laughter. "It was not quite England-cool, but the sun did not beat so fiercely, and we were able to escape our amah and play outside without baking. That was where I first met my wife."

"Maya."

"Yes, Maya." He shook his head as if to dispel the memories her name brought back to him. "But enough of her. Let's go find that Punch and Judy show I promised you. There will be one somewhere around, for sure, on a warm day like today."

In a quiet corner of the park next to the sand, and away from the noise of the brass band, they found the red-and-white-striped Punch and Judy show they were looking for. As they walked up, the puppet master finished the show to a round of cheers and the clatter of pennies from the spectators.

Caroline's face fell as he pulled the green baize curtain shut and the children drifted away in all directions, like ripples from a stone cast into a pond. "Never mind," she said, tugging on his arm, urging him away from the tent. "It will be an hour or more before he sets up again. We can always see one another day."

Dominic could feel the disappointment radiating from her, though she did not voice a word of complaint. Stepping up to the puppet master, he pressed a couple of golden guineas into the man's hand. "My wife would very much like to see your show."

With a payment such as that, the Punch and Judy man was only too happy to set up his theater again.

Out came the puppet master's assistant, the bottler, banging on his drum and playing on the pan pipes to draw another audience.

Her face beaming with delight, Caroline took possession of a beach chair and leaned forward to watch. Another group of children dragging parents or nursemaids by the hand materialized out of nowhere and gathered around, sitting crosslegged on the sand, their eyes wide with excitement.

Out came Punch swinging his little puppet stick and making a puppet fist. Judy in her nightgown and nightcap toddled out next, with a crying baby in her arms.

Punch complained about the noise, but the baby would not be pacified.

Thwack on the head of the baby went his stick. "That's the way to do it," Punch cried out gleefully as Judy ran away, the baby's cries having been silenced.

Out came Judy once again, brandishing a rolling pin at

Punch. Round and round the stage they chased each other, until *thwack* went Punch's stick on her head. "That's the way to do it," he called out as she dropped to the ground.

The doctor came to visit her, but *thwack* went Punch's stick on his head, and he, too, fell to the ground.

Next was the policeman puppet, chasing Punch around with a truncheon in his hand. Round and round they went until finally the policeman rapped Punch smartly on the head with his truncheon and Punch fell to the ground as if dead. The policeman dragged Punch off to jail and locked him up in a cell.

Out came the hangman to see Punch hanged for his crimes. "That's the way to do it," Punch called out in his shrill voice as he thwacked the hangman on his head and ran away laughing.

Old Nick came to fetch Punch away to Hell for his crimes, but not even the devil himself could stand up to Punch's stick. *Thwack* went Punch's stick on the devil's head, and Old Nick fell to the ground, vanquished by the triumphant Punch.

"Hurrah, hurrah, I've killed the devil!" Punch cried, clapping his hands together and dancing around the stage.

Dominic could not help laugh along with the rest of the spectators. Punch was so outlandishly silly, and his actions even more so. And most of all he laughed to see Caroline so happy, so engrossed in the action that the reserve she always showed with him melted away to nothing.

Their trip to the seaside was proving a success. That piece of her that she kept hidden, the part of her that concealed what the real Caroline was thinking and feeling, was slowly coming out of hiding and revealing itself to him. For the first time he felt that he was beginning to get to know the real woman behind the mask she wore every day.

He wasn't even sure why getting behind her mask had become so important to his peace of mind, but somehow or other it had become the driving force in his life. He was no longer content with her lush body and her obedience to his every whim. He wanted to get to know her soul.

Caroline lingered in her beach chair until the show was well and truly over and the puppet master had finished packing away his stage. Reluctantly she rose from her chair and took his arm once again. "That was quite magical. It was a real Punch and Judy show, with Punch thwacking everyone on the head and running away laughing, just like I remembered it from my childhood when Mama was still alive." She reached up on tiptoe and quickly planted a chaste kiss on his cheek. "Thank you."

He would pay a hundred puppet masters for the sake of one of Caroline's kisses given to him so freely. Though she was always ready to fulfill his every desire, it was seldom she volunteered a sign of affection of her own accord. Her usual reserve made this kiss doubly precious to him.

Just as they were wandering away from the tent, a group of gentlemen stumbled by in striped trousers and top hats, laughing and talking among themselves with great noise and gusto.

One of them cried out to Dominic in recognition. "Mr. Savage, old boy, what are you doing in Torquay?"

Dominic stiffened at the sound of the voice, recognizing it instantly despite the slur. It was Henry Thackeray, an acquaintance of his from the City, and obviously not as sober as he could be.

The whole group of them weaved their way over to where he stood arm in arm with Caroline.

"Meet my friends, Savage, old boy," Thackeray cried. His voice slurred a little from the drink and his gait was decidedly unsteady. "Edward Bartles, you know him I'm sure. He's a big man in the City. Just like you, eh, Dom."

Dominic did know him, by reputation more than anything. He was said to hold a grudge for less cause and for longer than any other man in London. And Bartles bore him a grudge for walking out of his dinner party with so little ceremony. He nodded his head brusquely. "Bartles."

Bartles's eyes narrowed in dislike. "Savage."

"And Sir Oliver Pickering. He comes drinking with us for all that he's a knight 'cause he ain't got two guineas to rub together, eh, do you now, old Pickles?"

"It is true I find my estate rather encumbered at present," Sir Pickering replied gravely, spoiling the gravity of his words with a loud hiccup.

"And old Warning here. An old friend of mine I haven't

seen since my school days. I met him here quite by chance. That's why we're celebrating so early in the day. You want to come join us?" He turned to the rest of his group. "Old Savage should join us, eh? The more the merrier, I always say."

With the exception of Bartles, the others assented loudly, with cries of "Bring him along" and "There's enough gin for twenty more."

Dominic shook his head. "I'm afraid I will have to pass on your invitation. I have a lady with me."

Thackeray peered owlishly at him and blinked several times. "By Jove, so you do. I didn't see her there. Your servant, ma'am." And he executed a tipsy bow.

"I didn't know you were married," Bartles said slyly, his face a picture of malice. "Congratulations must be in order, I presume." He doffed his hat with a sarcastic flourish. "To you and your lady wife."

Caroline's hand tightened convulsively on Dominic's arm but she did not speak.

"May I introduce you to Miss Caroline Clemens," he said tightly.

Sir Pickering swept his hat off in a courtly bow. "Delighted to make your acquaintance, fair lady."

"Charmed, I'm sure." This from Mr. Warning.

Thackeray was less politic in his appreciation. "What a stunner."

Bartles took her hand and held it a fraction too long for

politeness. "The late Isaac Clemens's daughter, aren't you? I haven't seen you since your father passed away. Where have you been hiding yourself?"

Caroline pulled her hand away from his grip, wiping it surreptitiously on the fabric of her gown. "I have been in mourning for my father."

"Ah, I see. Of course you have been," Bartles said, looking from her to Dominic with a calculating glance, taking in his possessive air and the fine cut of her gown, his voice as smooth and slippery as slime.

If Bartles said another word, Dominic thought, he would punch the man in the face and start a brawl on the spot. "Now, if you will excuse us. Miss Clemens and I have some business to conduct."

Caroline was still shaking well after they had left the group behind. He wanted to kill Thackeray, the stupid sot, and the rest of the drunken crew, for daring to make so free with her. She was a lady through and through and she deserved none of their familiarities, or Bartles's veiled insults.

He breathed deeply, containing his anger, not wanting to make Caroline feel any more uncomfortable than she already was. "I apologize on behalf of my friends," he said tightly. "They were insufferably rude."

"It doesn't matter. They did not mean any harm."

He would not allow her to brush their behavior under the carpet. "They insulted you."

"What did they say that I did not deserve?" She shrugged, but her voice was tight with anger. "I am not a lady, Dominic. I am your mistress, as Mr. Bartles made so clear he knew. They owe me no more politeness than they would owe a common whore."

"It would be easier for you if you were not with me."

"I do not regret the choices I have made, Dominic. Neither did I mean to imply that I was in any way unhappy with our bargain. Escaping the workhouse was worth a lifetime's worth of such petty insults. From most people they would not bother me." She hesitated. "It is just when I meet with people such as Mr. Thackeray and Mr. Bartles—respectable people who knew my father in happier times, who six months ago would have treated me with the respect they reserve for their own wives and daughters—I still find it . . . difficult."

They walked in silence for a while. Dominic's conscience troubled him. He had not truly realized before that his protection would not be sufficient to save Caroline from the insults of small-minded and pompous little fools like Bartles. Or that Bartles would take such malicious and ill-bred delight in causing her embarrassment.

Most of all he had not realized that Caroline would care so much for the strictures of a society that had abandoned her to a lingering death in the workhouse. "Do you not see any of your old friends anymore?" he asked.

"None of them."

"I had thought you would be out visiting your old acquaintances while I am at work in the City."

"I do not have anyone to visit. None of my previous acquaintances would welcome me into their houses. I would not embarrass them by calling on them uninvited."

Had it been him, he would have faced them all down and dared them to think what they liked, but it was different for a woman like Caroline, he supposed. In becoming his mistress, she had forever put herself beyond the pale of her former society. Until this moment he had not realized just how much. He may have saved her from starvation, but in doing so he had cut her off from all her former friends. And thinking about starvation, he realized that it was long past their usual hour for luncheon. He wasn't doing such a good job at saving her from starvation today, either. "Are you hungry?"

"Famished," she admitted. "Walking by the seaside has given me an appetite."

"We could find a nice seafood restaurant, or we could eat fish and chips on the pier. What do you fancy?"

"It seems a shame to waste the sunshine." Her smile had lost most of its strain. "Let's have fish and chips on the pier."

Ten minutes later, each of them carrying a bundle of steaming fish and chips wrapped in paper, they meandered over to a park bench with a pleasant view of the sea. Caroline plucked out a fragrant chip and popped it into her mouth. "I'm not sure why, but food always tastes better if you eat it with your fingers."

He had to agree with her. The fish was fresh and melted in his mouth, and the chips were crispy and golden. They sat quietly in the sunshine, eating their way through their lunch.

When the fish and chips were gone, they continued to walk, lazily now that they were full of food.

An itinerant photographer was peddling his wares on the sand, touting his skill and the technical wonders of his camera, invented in the Americas and able to produce a finished photograph within mere moments.

Dominic quickened his pace. "I want a photograph of you." He wanted to capture this day forever in an image that would carry these precious memories with it. A cheap tintype image, it may be, but an image that lovers everywhere had taken by the seaside.

Spotting a likely customer heading in his direction, the traveling salesman, a short balding man in a waistcoat of violent yellow, bent all his eloquence on the pair of them. "You'll be wanting a portrait now, will you? A picture of the two of you together, perhaps?" He gave them a knowing wink. "I won't take more than a moment, and I'll have a picture for you to take home with you and treasure for the rest of your days."

Dominic seated Caroline on the beach chair set out for the purpose and stood back. "A photograph of Mrs. Clemens, if you please."

"You won't regret, sir, I can promise you that. I've got the finest quality camera this side of the Atlantic, and it takes the sharpest, most true-to-life pictures you ever saw. You won't find another one in Torquay like it."

Caroline arranged her skirts around her, a slight frown on her face. The sunlight glinted off her hair, making the soft brown gleam with a golden sheen. Her hands were clasped tightly together in her lap and her back was stiff.

"There's nothing to be nervous about," the salesman said, adjusting his equipment. "It doesn't hurt a bit. You won't feel a thing. Now, give your husband a pretty smile."

A tremulous smile crossed her face, but it did not reach her eyes.

"Excellent. Now hold still." With a practiced motion, he slid a panel on his contraption sideways. "There, that's it. That looked not too bad, if I say so myself. You're very wise to get your photograph taken in the autumn like this, rather than in the harsh light of summer. The light is quite perfect for photography at this time of year. I shall have a photograph fit for the Queen herself in just a few moments."

With hardly an interruption to his patter, he produced a thin sheet of metal with Caroline's likeness captured on it. "See, look at that quality. You won't find many as good as that, no siree. And what a pretty likeness it is, too. A lovely picture like that and just two shillings to take it away with you. A bargain, sir, a bargain, and it would be at twice the price."

Dominic handed him a couple of shillings and took the picture. Superficially the photograph had captured her likeness well enough, but it had missed the sparkle in her eyes and the lightness of her step. It had drawn only the outward show, and missed everything that was quintessentially Caroline.

Still, he tucked it away into its case with care. If he were to be fair, no photograph in the world could ever capture what he saw in Caroline, her strength and her courage.

"And how about a picture of you, sir, for the lady?" the salesman continued. "Surely the lady would like a keepsake of this outing the same as you would." He turned to Caroline with entreaty. "Only two shillings for a lovely picture for you to keep next to your heart. Surely your husband wouldn't deny you such a simple pleasure."

She put her hand up to ward off his entreaties. "I do not need a photograph. Not when I have his face in front of me to look at every day."

The salesman turned back to him. "No picture for your wife? For shame, sir. What will keep her company on those long, lonely nights when you are away on business if she doesn't have a likeness of you to prop up beside her bed?"

He was about to shake his head and move on when he caught a glimpse of the look of naked longing in Caroline's eyes. For whatever reason, she wanted a tintype of him and she wanted it very badly indeed. He could see her desire in her eyes, though she hadn't uttered a word.

He seated himself on the chair she had just vacated, only just managing to suppress his smile. She must have some softer feelings for him, or she would not want a picture of him. For all her serenity, she had feelings hidden deep inside her that sometimes had to bubble to the surface.

His photograph once taken, he handed it to her with a smile. "A small memento of Torquay."

She accepted it graciously, in the spirit in which it was given.

Only because he was watching her closely did he notice the care with which she tucked it away into her reticule.

He took her arm again with a feeling of triumph. His tactics were working. Caroline was his. All his.

Though she might fight against it, he would make her admit the truth. He was more than her master, her protector, the man who bought her clothes and jewelry and provided the house for her to live in. He was more than her bed partner at night, more than the man who made her cry out in ecstasy with his skillful fingers and tongue.

With that one glimpse into her soul, he knew the truth. He was her lover, her soul mate, the other half of her.

It was dark by the time they reached Sugar and Spice once again. Dominic handed Caroline out of the carriage, the tintype, carefully wrapped in brown paper and tied with string, under his arm.

Mrs. Bertram met them just inside the door and handed him a telegram tucked into an envelope. "This came for you this afternoon. The boy had been instructed to stay for an answer, but he left again when I told him you were out for the day. I promised I would pass it to you as soon as you arrived home."

With a brief nod of thanks, he took the envelope and stuck it into his waistcoat pocket without opening it. There would be time enough for business in the morning. Tonight belonged to him, and to Caroline.

"You must be weary after your long journey," Mrs. Bertram said as she ushered them up the stairs. "I will have some supper brought to your room as soon as may be."

Once alone in their bedroom, Caroline embraced Dominic with tenderness he had not experienced from her before. Her embrace was gentle, the rubbing of her hands over his back questing, as if she was discovering him for the first time. Tilting her head up, she kissed him full on the mouth. "I had a lovely day today," she said as she broke away once again, her hands moving to his chest to unbutton his jacket and shirt. "Thank you for the excursion."

He gasped in pleasure as she ran her hands over his chest, her fingernails raking his sensitive nipples. It was definitely time to get naked with her, as he had thought about doing all day.

Breaking their embrace, he removed his jacket and shirt, followed by his shoes and socks. He paused for a moment to watch as Caroline followed his lead, removing her dress as quickly as she could, then starting on her undergarments.

She glanced at him, a mischievous look in her eye as she dragged her chemise over her head. "Race you."

"Is that a challenge?"

She tossed her stockings on the floor. "Winner gets a kiss."

One of Caroline's kisses was a prize worth having. Intent on winning, he hopped around on one leg while pulling off his trousers, nearly falling disastrously into the fireplace in his haste. The poker and tongs fell with a clatter onto the hearth, sending a puff of soot into the air.

Giggling at his curses, Caroline flung off the last of her clothes, losing the competition by a pair of pantaloons.

Naked at last, he pulled her on top of him onto the bed. "So, how about my kiss, then?"

Their kiss was just starting to heat up when there was a knock at the door and a voice called out to them from the hallway. "Your supper is here."

With a mad dash, they scrambled under the covers and pulled them up to their chins. As the door opened, Caroline ducked right under the blankets.

A maid entered, a tray in her hands. "Cold meats and a pot of tea, sir."

Just then he felt a warm mouth engulf his cock. "Just on the sideboard, please," he said, covering up his choke of surprise with a fake cough.

The maid put the tray on the sideboard and stepped back, dusting her hands together. "Is there anything else I can get for you, sir?"

"No, nothing, thank you."

Still, she seemed in a mood to linger. "Did you have a nice day, sir?"

Under the blankets Caroline continued pleasuring his cock, massaging his balls while running her tongue around the head. "Very nice," he replied, his breath in his throat. Whether he was referring to the day they had spent by the seaside or the warmth of Caroline's mouth on his cock, he could not have said.

"Torquay, wasn't it?"

Before he could answer, he felt Caroline take his cock in her hand and rub vigorously up and down, bringing him close to orgasm as he tried to frame his answer. "Yes. Torquay . . . nice weather . . . Punch and Judy . . ." was the best he could muster as Caroline pumped his cock hard and fast.

The maid's eyes lit up. "Ah, Punch and Judy. I love them shows. Can't recall the last time I saw one."

Mercifully, Caroline had stopped the exquisite torture of her hand at his cock and was now merely licking lightly up and down his hard shaft.

"Thank you for the supper," he said, finally managing to get out a coherent sentence. "I shall be sure to ring if I need anything else."

Taking the hint, the maid at last left.

As soon as the door closed behind her, he flung back the covers to reveal a smug-looking Caroline curled up on the sheets. "You'll be sorry you did that, young lady!"

With that he pinned her down with his weight, tickling her until he was concerned her shrieks would bring company again. "Do you surrender?"

"No!"

"Then it will have to be punishment of a different kind." Releasing his weight from her, he sat up and spread her legs, then slid down her body to tease the top of her wet pussy with his tongue, lapping lightly at the nub of her clit. That brought cries of a different kind as he gently eased two fingers into her cunt, rubbing upward to her sensitive place.

Softly, he heard, "I surrender."

With her acquiescence, he stopped teasing her pussy and slid back up her body, kissing as he went. Finally he reached her mouth, his tongue questing as she opened to him.

He shifted his weight and slid his cock easily into her cunt, her hips raised to meet his thrusts, her pleasure heightened with the pressure on her clit.

With his cock deep inside her, he looked into her eyes as he continued a slow rhythm. Her gaze met his, and their world shrunk until there was nothing but the two of them. Their breathing matched their rhythm as the climax built. Just before they both reached their peak he came to a stop, his breath slowing as he continued to gaze into her eyes.

He remained motionless for what seemed forever until Caroline started to lightly massage his back, up and down in long, languid strokes. Eventually she cupped his ass and pulled him to her, as deep as he could go. She raised her legs and entwined them about his back, beginning again the long rhythm that this time brought her to orgasm.

With her arms and legs about him she squeezed as her climax shuddered through her body, bringing him to a peak of intensity that locked his muscles in absolute pleasure. It was as if the two of them had merged into one, their bodies and spirits closer than he had ever experienced with any other lover.

They lay together in their tight embrace for several minutes. With Caroline holding him so close, he felt as if she were keeping him from escaping, afraid that he would somehow disappear in a puff of smoke like a fakir at the fair.

After a timeless moment he rolled onto his side and brought the eiderdown over them both. Hugging close to her, he cupped her breast protectively in his hand as he fell asleep.

Not until they were on the train the following morning and well on the way back to London did Dominic remember the telegram in his pocket.

He pulled it out, wondering what was so urgent that it necessitated the expense of a telegram. His man of business, Arnold Turfrey, was more than capable of taking care of things in his absence. In fact, Turfrey had positively encouraged him to go away on this latest jaunt, swearing that his business was left in good hands and that he would deal with any issues that might arise.

To his surprise, the telegram was from his lawyer rather than his man of business. He opened it with a growing sense of unease. Though an honest man, his lawyer did not have

Turfrey's business acumen and was only peripherally involved in his business dealings.

He read the telegram once and then again, not believing the words that were spelled out in black and white. Was it possible that he had been so blind? That he could have been so easily misled in the essential character of a man?

His stomach churned uncomfortably, and for the first time the rollicking motion of the train made him sick to his stomach. Mumbling an incoherent excuse to Caroline, he lurched into the water closet and emptied his stomach. Over and over again.

Even that did not make him feel much better. Though his stomach was still churning away inside, he rinsed out his mouth first with water and then with a swig of brandy before rejoining Caroline in the carriage. "It's nothing. Just the motion of the train," he said in response to her worried inquiry. "It made me feel ill all of a sudden. That's all."

He lay back on the sofa as she fetched a cloth, dipped it in cool water, and wiped his face. Her hands were cool and the attention gradually soothed his stomach, if not his spirit.

Surely his lawyer was mistaken, had blown a small incident out of all proportion, and even now was waiting for him at the office with an explanation and an apology for causing him a moment's concern.

It was not losing the money that worried him the most. His fortune had been easily made and he knew it could just as easily be lost again with one turn on Fortune's wheel. Fortune was capricious—another turn of the wheel and once again he would be on top.

He just did not want to lose Fortune's favor now, when Caroline's heart was within his grasp.

The loss of his wealth terrified him only because of what it would mean to her. His fists clenched at his sides. God, but he didn't think he could bear it if he were to lose her now.

Before he knew it, the train was pulling into Victoria Station. Still feeling ill and shaky, he fetched their bags and then bundled Caroline into a hansom cab. "I won't be coming home with you. I have to go into the office. I will be home later tonight. Don't wait up for me."

Her anxious face, so pale and beautiful, stared back up at him through the window of the cab. "Is everything all right?"

"Just fine," he lied, contorting his face into the semblance of a smile. There was no point in worrying her before he knew all the facts. He would not despair just yet. There might yet be some way of salvaging the situation.

He stood in the road and stared helplessly after her as the cab trundled away, before turning around and striding off in the direction of his office in the City. If even half of what the telegram had conveyed to him was true, that would be one of the last times he would get to look at her face.

Caroline rode back in the hansom cab in silence. For all Dominic's brave words, she knew that something was wrong. Very wrong indeed.

The telegram had been the cause of his sudden sickness on the train, and of his preoccupied air for the rest of the journey home. It must have brought him the worst of news.

The look in his eyes of mingled despair and disbelief was exactly like her father's had been when his business empire had shattered. It had sent tentacles of horror snaking through her body. No man looked like that unless his fondest dreams had been utterly destroyed.

And when a man's dreams were destroyed, what was left for him but death? Her father had taught her that harsh lesson.

If Dominic was ruined, would he seek the same way out of his troubles as her father had?

Dominic had told her not to wait up for him, but she could not go to bed. She could not even bear to remove her traveling gown and slip into a dressing gown. When the bad news came for her later that evening, as she was sure it would, she wanted to face it fully dressed.

Maybe she was fretting herself all for nothing, but she could not make herself believe such a comforting lie.

Her escape from poverty and despair had been too easy to be real. Dominic had come riding into her life like a white knight, and she had allowed herself to be rescued. She had allowed herself to believe that her family was not marked out for misfortune, that they would be able to recover from the devastating blow they had been dealt. In the secret recesses of her heart she had even allowed herself to hope that one day, somehow, she would find happiness.

As the light faded and the night fell, and slowly the sounds of day were extinguished to make way for the subtler and more mysterious sounds of the night, she sat stiff-backed in the chair, her hands folded in her lap, and waited for the axe to fall.

Eleven

Dominic hailed the cab and settled into it for a dismal ride home. The telegram from his lawyer had understated, rather than overstated, the extent of the problem. And now it looked as though it was too late to do anything about it.

Arnold Turfrey, his trusted partner and business manager, had ruined him. Worse than that, he had deceived and betrayed him. And for so little gain.

It could not hurt any worse if Turfrey had taken a knife and plunged it into his ribs and twisted it viciously in the wound.

The accounts had been cleverly manipulated for months to hide the small losses that Turfrey had been making in stock purchases and sales. Purchases and sales that he should never have been making with company money in the first place.

Then, just a fortnight ago, Turfrey had bought stock in

what he clearly thought was a sure thing, in the hopes of recouping all the money he had lost over the last year.

The purchase had gone disastrously wrong. Unable to face up to what he had done and take the consequences, he had compounded his folly. He had cleaned out every penny that was still left in the company accounts and fled. Probably to his family in Italy, the lawyer suspected, or possibly Greece.

At any rate, Dominic's business was ruined, all his ready cash was gone, and he was left with debts that the sale of all his remaining assets would only just cover.

He was ruined. Utterly and inescapably ruined. And all for the sake of Turfrey's foolish greed and incompetence.

He did not mind so much for himself, but for Caroline. Even if she were to fancy herself a little fond of him, as he had lately suspected she did, she could not stay with him now. He could offer her nothing, not even a decent home to live in. What woman worth her salt would stay on such slim prospects as that? He could not ask her to make such a sacrifice.

The lights were still on in the parlor when he arrived home, weary and sore at heart. Caroline must have waited up for him after all.

He stumbled into the parlor and sank onto the sofa. Her face, though pale, was composed, but her back was unnaturally straight and she did not look surprised to see him collapse exhausted on the couch.

He shut his eyes so he could not see the hurt in her eyes when he gave her the news. Though the temptation to wait and tell her in the morning was strong, he thought it was better to face her now than later. The news would not get any better if he delayed until the morning. And the more he brooded on it, the worse it would be to tell her.

"You are late, Dominic." Her voice was soft, calm, with no accusation in it.

He opened his eyes again and sat up straight. There was no help for it. He had to face his future like a man, not like a sniveling coward. He would not run from the unpleasant truth as Turfrey had done, hiding away in Italy to avoid having to see the consequences of his embezzling. Hiding from the truth would make him no better than the man he despised.

No, he was better than that. Still, he had best confess while his courage ran strong in his veins. "I am ruined, Caroline." The thought of losing her, of seeing her walk away from him and into the arms of another man who would be able to give all the things that he was no longer able to give her, made him feel green. He swallowed the bile that rose up in his throat. Now was not the time to show such weakness.

"Ruined?" She nodded once, as if confirming to herself what she already suspected. "Completely ruined?"

"Not completely." He gave a wry smile. "There is enough left of the ruins of my fortune to keep me out of the poor-house. But that is all. I will have to sell this house, dismiss the staff, and start all over again. If I live frugally, I will have enough to pay off all my creditors and have a pittance left to finance my next new venture." He ran his hands through his hair distractedly. "God willing, it will prove to be more worthwhile than the last one."

"You will not be destitute, then. I am glad of it. That is an uncomfortable situation to find yourself in."

She was taking the news calmly. Too calmly. "You understand what I am saying, Caroline? I cannot afford to keep you any longer. I have no money for expensive presents or holidays in the country. Not even enough to run a decent establishment. I will have to let you go."

Her face was white as milk, but her expression was as serene as ever. "Of course I understand. You have no obligation to me. I was expecting nothing more."

She was worthy to be the consort to a king. He could not ask her to share his poverty. Never had he been more glad of the ruthless bargain she had struck with him at the beginning of their liaison. Her property in Hertfordshire had escaped the wreck of his fortunes. His lawyer had put it in her name just in the nick of time to save it from Turfrey's predations. Given that it was no longer his, none of his creditors had a single claim on it. Her future, at least, was assured. Whatever happened to him, she would not die in a ditch from cold and hunger. "You are young and beautiful. You will find another protector." The words did violence to his soul. "Once it is known that I have had to give you up, the vultures will be circling around you in no time."

"I'm sure they will be."

"You will not suffer financially from my loss. Everything

that I made over to you is still yours. No one can touch it."

"Are you going to shoot yourself?"

Her calm words, and the calm manner in which she spoke them, sent chills running through his body. Was death so familiar to her that she could talk about it so calmly? Did she really think he would take the coward's way out of his troubles? "What kind of a question is that?"

Her face turned pale pink at the vehemence in his voice. "A reasonable one, under the circumstances, I should think. After all, plenty of men have found a similar escape. My own father included."

"I do not intend to find peace at the wrong end of a pistol."

"I would not judge you if you wanted to take such a way out of your difficulties. I nearly did. That night when I first met you at Mrs. Finsbury's soiree." Her brittle laugh cut through to his very soul. "That is why I allowed you to take me in the conservatory. I had already decided that we should all die, and I thought it would matter little enough if I disposed of my virginity first. But my courage didn't last. There were plenty of moments in the workhouse when I wished I had had to courage to kill us all as I had intended."

"What stopped you?" He could not help but ask, ghoulish as the topic was. She had never before even hinted at her reason for allowing him to seduce her in the conservatory. And he had been so glad to find her again that he had not thought to tackle her reserve on the matter. More concerned about the future than the past, he had wanted only to secure her as his mistress, and not to scare her off by probing too deeply into her previous life.

"The noise of the pistol cocking woke Teddy up. He opened his eyes and looked at me and told me he was not afraid to die."

That was her secret, the key to her soul. "But you could not do it." Whatever she may have planned in her darkest moment, she was no murderess. How ironic that he had stumbled on her secret just when she was about to leave him forever. He had the key, but there was no longer any treasure chest for him to open. He had lost his right even to try.

"I could not shoot him when he was awake. I misfired, shot into the floor instead. And that woke all the others and by then my courage was gone."

She had known what was coming, then, when she had taken her siblings to the workhouse, and thought to escape it the only way that had been left to her. From the bottom of his heart he thanked Teddy's light sleeping. Had he known that evening that Caroline was walking away from him with such murderous feelings in her heart, he would never have allowed her to leave.

"So now you know the worst of me, the reason why I could never condemn another man for taking his own life." She gave an uneasy shrug. "I have been too close to that desperation myself to blame you if you chose that way out."

He could at least set her mind at ease on that score, and ease her mind from the worry of seeing him hanging from the chandelier or lying on the floor of his study in a pool of blood when she came down for breakfast in the morning. "My circumstances are not as desperate as that, not as desperate as your father's were. True, I have lost most of what I have made over the years, but no matter. I am young and energetic enough to start all over again, and too proud to let one small setback defeat me. My straitened means are only temporary, I can assure you."

At least he hoped they were only temporary. It would take a run of excellent luck to lift him from his poverty again. Luck, and a lot of hard work. "It is just that in the meantime, much as I would like to, I cannot afford to keep you."

"It is late now," she said, "but I will not trouble you any longer than necessary. I shall leave for Hertfordshire in the morning."

He bowed his head, covering his face with his hands to his anguish. Her calm acceptance of his decision only made it worse. He had thought that maybe she was growing fond of him in his own right, that he meant more to her than the presents he made and the gifts he gave. How wrong he had been about her. Indifferent to the core, she did not care a fig for him or his troubles.

Her serenity was proof of her utter indifference to him, when all he could think of was his hopeless, unrequited love for her. "The carriage will be at your disposal until noon to take you to the station. After that, I am afraid, it will be gone." Better men than he was had lost their hearts to a courtesan and survived. He would, too, no matter that it felt like his soul was being ripped screaming from his body.

Hertfordshire was, if anything, colder and grayer than London.

At any other time in her life Caroline would have gloried in the estate that was now hers, with its small but comfortable country house and the acres of good farmland that went with it. The house was not as grand as Dominic's town house nor as large as her father's house had been, but it was hers, all hers. She had earned the right to be here, and nobody could take that right away from her.

The land itself, however, did not look to be in the best shape. Even through the haze of depression that settled on her after she had left Dominic in London, she knew instantly that it had been badly run. Her examination of the estate records confirmed her first impression. Someone, she was quite sure, was skimming the profits that the place ought to be making, stripping the place bare instead of reinvesting for future growth.

Judging by the shifty look in his eyes and the way he would not meet her gaze, the steward was well aware of his failings. And she quickly learned from the servants' grapevine that his wife had aspirations above her station, and he was keeping a pretty young girl on the side, as well. Two terrible temptations to cook the books.

Though he tried to bluster about the last harvest being poor and not having enough money to modernize his agricultural techniques sufficiently, he folded quickly enough in the face of her stiff-backed determination.

His attitude made her smile. She had faced far worse things in her life than a lazy and dishonest steward who deserved to be transported as a thief. Did he really expect that just because she was a woman, she would crumble under a few harsh words? If he had not stolen so much of hers, and Dominic's, money, she would have been tempted to laugh.

As it was, she simply informed him in no uncertain tones that he was now dismissed and he had until the end of the week to clear his belongings off her property. Though he alternately sulked and stormed, by the end of the week he was gone.

The rest of the household staff, seeing how quickly she had dealt with the steward, gave her little trouble. Their minor depredations into used tea leaves and candle ends she could live with—they were the accepted perks of staff in a large household—but she would not tolerate any pilfering on a larger scale.

This estate was hers, and she had to run it well. Teddy and Dorothea's school fees had been paid for the term, but in a few weeks she would have to find the money for the next term's fees. They depended on her. She would not let them down, or have them worry about the family finances yet again. They had faced enough hardship and done enough worrying for a lifetime.

It was not just the school fees that concerned her. Any hope of dowries for her older sisters had gone the way of the rest of

Dominic's fortune. If they were to have any hope of marrying, she would have to pay them each a dowry out of the savings she could make from the farm. The weight of the pigs in the piggery and the length of wool on the backs of her sheep took on a personal meaning for her. They were Teddy's hope of a profession and her sisters' hopes of a family of their own.

As the days wore on, the heaviness of her heart was not lifted by being in charge of her own household once again. Though she had everything running smoothly in the house, and was fast learning how to run the farm on top of that, she was not happy. The autumn weather was cold and damp, and no matter how many heated bricks she had placed in her bed of an evening, she could not get warm. She missed Dominic's solid presence in the bed beside her, she missed the feel of his body pressed against hers, she missed his strength and the protection he lent her. And most of all, she missed his kindness.

For he *had* been good to her while it lasted. Though she had been hurt to the quick by the speed with which he cast her off when he got into financial difficulties, still, he had been kind to her.

After all, he owed her nothing more. They'd had only the semblance of a relationship, a faint shadow of the real thing. Nobody knew that better than she, who had bargained for everything that he had given her. But now that it was over and they had parted, she would have given a good deal to have that semblance back again.

Sunday afternoons were the worst, she decided, as she sat disconsolately in the parlor, going over the accounts for the week. The weather was so bleak that although it was barely past noon, she had already lit a gas lamp to help her make out the figures. Despite the coal fire in the grate, the room was damp and cold and she shivered as she worked. There was nothing worse than being cold when one was trying to do accounts. The figures refused to add up.

The sound of carriage wheels roused her from her reverie. Visitors were scarce at this time of year when the days were short and the roads muddy. Besides, she had been so busy with running the farm that she had spent little time cultivating the acquaintance of her neighbors. They would cut her dead if they knew her real situation. She had no wish to cultivate such shallow relationships as they could offer her.

At first she didn't recognize the man who was ushered into her parlor.

Her visitor noticed her confusion and blushed beet red. "Henry Thackeray at your service, ma'am. We met before. In Torquay."

Henry Thackeray was short and square, and sported massive sideburns that crawled across his face like whiskery black caterpillars. She remembered now. How could she have forgotten the drunken men who had accosted Dominic, and then her, in such a familiar fashion?

Inwardly she groaned, guessing at the reason behind his visit. She ought to accept him, she knew she ought to, but the thought was distasteful in the extreme. Though he was a wealthy banker and could no doubt afford his own personal laundress should he choose, his linen smelled none too clean. She could not abide slovenly habits in a man.

Still, she invited him to sit down, and chose a seat as far away from him as was consistent with politeness. The sour, slightly acrid smell of his unwashed body pervaded the room, mixing unpleasantly with the dampness and the smoke from the coal fire.

"Miss Clemens, or may I call you Caroline?" he continued without waiting for an answer, not giving her a chance to object to his use of her Christian name. "I imagine you are surprised to see me here."

She bowed her head in acknowledgment. "I was wondering how you found me." Content for the time being to be left entirely alone, she had not advertised her retreat to Hertfordshire. Indeed, she had been hastened off too quickly to advertise it even had she wanted to.

"I ran into Dominic in town and heard of the reversal of his fortunes." He shook his head, setting his sideburns waving. "I told him that he should stay right away from that last investment, the one that ruined him, but it seems he took no notice. Foolish boy. You can imagine that my thoughts immediately ran to you, left alone and friendless again." He smiled at her, showing all his teeth. "Dominic told me where I could find you, hiding out in the countryside. So I hopped onto the train right away and came up here to let you know that there was at least one man left in the world who cared about what happened to you."

Caroline sat in silence, allowing him to rattle on at her about all the advantages that a liaison with him would entail for her. She supposed she should be glad that she had another customer to buy the meager wares she had to sell, but the only emotion she could manage to summon up was a rather bored distaste. She could not imagine even kissing Mr. Thackeray, let alone welcoming him into her bed. Her body shuddered with revulsion at the mere idea.

"...my wife will not object to our liaison, I can assure you, or make any trouble for you over it. She has everything a woman wants—a couple of fine children in the nursery, a fine house with enough servants to keep it that way, and plenty of pin money for new gloves. I shall keep her sweet with a new dress once in a while. She will be perfectly content with that." He made an odd face. "I doubt she will even notice that I have ceased to visit her bed."

She could not do it. Not even for the sake of Teddy's school fees. She would scrimp and save on the income from the estate and pay for them that way. Mr. Thackeray would never be her lover. It would demean them both. "It was kind of you to come so far to see me."

He beamed. "It was no trouble, Caroline. No trouble at all."

"But I could never accept so much from you. Not from a married man." It was the best excuse she could come up with on the spur of the moment. He had come all that way to see her, and it would be churlish of her to insult him for what he meant as a kindness. "If you were single, it would be a different matter." She allowed a disappointed sigh to escape her. "But I could never interfere between a man and his wife. It would not be right."

His face fell. "My wife married me for my money. She does not care for me in the least. I thought that you...that you might understand me."

Foolish man, to think that he could buy understanding. "No woman marries solely for money. She must have had a good deal of liking for you to accept your suit."

"Do you really think so?" The hope on his face was almost painful. Whatever had motivated his wife, poor Mr. Thackeray had not married for money. He was clearly still in love with his wife.

A sudden wave of pity swept over her. Poor man, to be wedded to a woman whom he loved but who did not return his affection. Perhaps she could do him a good turn. At any rate it would cost her nothing to try. "I cannot be your mistress, but you deserve some recompense for traveling all this way to offer me your support. Would you like me to teach you how to win your wife's love back again?"

He blinked at her as if he did not believe his ears. "You could...you would do that for me?"

"If you would like me to."

"I would like it above all things. But I had thought it impossible. That is why I decided..." His voice tailed off.

"That is why you decided to visit me."

"Exactly." He had the grace to look ashamed of himself.

Caroline rang the bell for afternoon tea. "Let me have a few moments to think," she said, scribbling some notes on the papers in front of her. "We can discuss this over a cup of tea."

"You wouldn't happen to have a drop of sherry in the house, would you?" he asked hopefully. "I prefer sherry in the afternoons."

"I'm sorry, I do not drink spirits," she said. "Women don't like spirits overmuch—or their effect on menfolk, either."

"There seem to be a good many things that women don't like," he grumbled as she scribbled. "Strong spirits, muddy boots, and a whole heap of other stuff. What about telling me a few things they do like instead?"

Caroline poured him a cup of the tea that had just arrived—it must have been sitting outside the door waiting for her to request it, it came so promptly. "A woman likes an active man. You must go for a walk every morning. A mile and a half at least." That would lessen his rather unattractive paunch and help to get rid of his unnatural pallor. Pale skin was all very well, but his looked as though he had just crawled out from under a rock.

His face paled still further at the prospect of so much exercise. "Every morning?" He looked doubtfully into his teacup, sipped a little, and made a face as if it tasted nasty.

"Every morning before breakfast. Then when you arrive home again, you must bathe and trim your whiskers and put on clean linen before you go to your work in the City." She was tempted to suggest that he shave his monstrous sideburns right off, but she didn't dare go too far all at once. A good trim would remove the worst of them, so he did not look quite so much like an unkempt werewolf.

This time he just looked puzzled at her suggestion. "Clean linen every morning? I only change it once a week, on Saturdays."

Ugh. Poor Mrs. Thackeray. The woman must be a saint to put up with her husband's disgusting habits. "Clean linen every morning," she repeated firmly. "Then when you return home, bathe and change your linen again when you dress for dinner."

"Fresh linen again before dinner?"

"There is nothing a woman likes better than the smell of clean linen."

"What a waste of linen," he grumbled. "I shall have to buy a ridiculous quantity of smalls. Wouldn't my wife like a nice pearl brooch instead of all this walking and clean clothes?"

"No doubt she would like a nice pearl brooch as well," Caroline said, "but that hasn't worked on its own, has it, or you wouldn't be here."

"I've bought her half a dozen pearl brooches," he admitted. "And none of them have made a jot of difference."

"Does your wife particularly like pearls?"

His face was a picture of confusion at her question. "Doesn't every woman?"

Poor man. He really did not have a clue about women. She was providing a public service in educating him. "I don't. Pearls are too bland and colorless—they have no life or fire. I much prefer emeralds. And there is a limit to the number of brooches any woman can wear in a lifetime."

She let the implication of her words sink in for a few moments and then continued with her lesson. "Then over dinnertime, ask your wife about her day, and listen—really listen—to her answers. Admire her new bonnet. Tell her how elegant she looks. And after dinner, help her to bathe the babies and put them to bed."

"Help bathe the babies?" He looked frankly horrified at this suggestion. "That's their nurse's duty. I wouldn't know how."

"Then it's time you learned...if you want to impress your wife, that is. And when you are in bed with her, you must take care to satisfy her needs as well as your own."

"But...but she is a respectable woman," he spluttered. "She doesn't have needs like that."

"Nonsense. All women do, respectable or not. It is up to a husband to discover how to first arouse and then to satisfy them."

His face was splotchy red with embarrassment. "You mean to say that all women..." His voice tailed off into a choke. "Even wives? Even Prudence?"

"Especially wives. They like to know how much they mean to their husbands. I would wager that your Prudence is no different."

He shook his head in amazement. "I never would have believed it. Do you really mean to tell me that all this ... this frippery, matters to a woman?"

"It all matters to a woman. If her heart is not made of stone, this will melt it."

He clapped his hat back on his head and made to leave, his tea still undrunk. "Thank you for your advice," he said, rather doubtfully. "I suppose I will try it. I have nothing to lose anyway," he muttered to himself as he walked distractedly back to his carriage.

Some courtesan she was, she thought wryly as she sat in the window seat and stared idly out at the rain dripping from the hedges. She'd only ever had one customer, and to her shame she had fallen in love with him. That was why she could not entertain any other offers to keep her, though she knew it would be in her best interest to find another protector as soon as may be. Farming was scarcely less uncertain than speculation. The crops could fail or the prices could drop and she would be left once again with nothing. Some fine pieces of jewelry to pawn when the going got rough, or a few elegant gowns that would fetch a decent price at a second-hand clothes shop, would keep her that much further away from disaster.

Just for that reason alone she should not have sent Mr. Thackeray away, for all that she did not like his sweaty palms and his thick waist. He had money and plenty of it. She was a courtesan—she ought to care more about the state of a man's pocketbook than about the state of his whiskers. But if she were to be honest with herself, all she truly cared about was Dominic.

That week, she entertained visitor after visitor, all of them on the same errand as Mr. Thackeray. Young Frederic Warning was sent happily on his way with a kiss on his cheek—enough to win him the wager he'd entered into with his friends from Oxford. Sir Oliver Pickering made her an offer which, considering the ruinous state of his pocketbook, was relatively generous, but it was not enough to tempt her to accept. Edward Bartles made it clear to her that he only wanted her because she had been Dominic's, and he was determined to acquire everything that had once belonged to Dominic. She treated him with the scorn that he deserved.

Captain Bellamy even had the effrontery to call to renew his penny-pinching offer. She had her footman throw him bodily out of the door and then had the dogs set loose on him. The sight of him scampering back to his carriage squealing with fright as the dogs snapped at his heels made her heart burn with gladness. When one of the dogs jumped up and ripped a patch off his trousers across his buttocks, her revenge felt truly complete, and she made a mental note to feed that dog an extra ration of fresh meat for supper.

The weeks passed, most days bringing one offer or another to tempt her. None of her callers were remotely suitable. They were all too young, too old, too poor, too mean, or too married. She could not accept any of them to fill Dominic's place in her bed.

But she was aware that her dithering was not going to fill her coffers. She needed to take another lover, and the sooner the better. Teddy's fees would not pay themselves, and if she were to see her sisters regularly, she needed to buy their train tickets. They could not afford to visit her on their less than lavish weekly wages.

And she already had plenty of other calls on her money. Her house badly needed reroofing, and a number of her tenants' cottages were due for repairs. A farm such as hers, she was finding, needed most of the profits ploughed back into it in order to keep it going.

She heaved a sigh. Owning a small country estate, though it gave her somewhere to live, was not the solution to her money worries as she had hoped it would be.

What she needed was a sponsor, a well-connected woman who could advertise her availability—discreetly, of course—and to all the right sort of men. She would be happy to pay a finder's fee to such a woman, if only she could locate one.

Her hostess at Sugar and Spice. Now there was an idea. Cornwall was too far and out of the way to attract enough bidders, but surely Mrs. Bertram would know of such women in London and be able to provide her with an introduction.

She would ask her at once, while her courage was still hot.

Sitting down at her writing desk, she began to pen a very delicate letter.

The Price of Desire

* * *

Dominic stood before the entrance of the unprepossessing coffeehouse in a shabby part of town—on the fringes of the business district, but not quite part of it. PALIMPSEST, proclaimed the sign painted over the door. From a quick glance through the grubby window, it appeared to be simply that, a coffeehouse. He could see a small handful of customers reading their newspapers while enjoying a brief respite from their day's work. One was eating a large chop, tucking into the fatty cut of meat with great gusto.

He looked once more at the invitation, carefully reading the address neatly written at the top of the card. Then he looked again at the street number in gold numerals placed beside the entrance before him. This had to be the place.

A small brass bell announced his presence as he opened the door and stepped inside.

With an uncharacteristic lack of confidence, he patted his coat pocket for the hundredth time, feeling the slim envelope that contained his offer to Caroline. A meager offer, for sure, but it was all he had.

It was, he thought without any hope whatsoever, his last chance to win her back.

A young serving girl in a clean and well-pressed gown of quality cotton approached him. "A table for one, sir? We have chops for a good price, if you're wanting a bite to eat." She was definitely better turned out than he would have expected in a simple coffeehouse in this part of town.

"I am here to see Mrs. Erskine." At her inquiring look, he held the card before him so the girl could read it. "I have an invitation."

The girl barely glanced at it. "You'll be one of Miss Clemens's gentlemen, then. Please follow me, sir."

He followed close on her heels, wanting to have this affair tidied away as soon as could be. As much as he might wish to, he could not change the course of events now. He would make his offer, Caroline would make her choice, and he would return to his dingy rooms, alone.

He would not torment himself with vain hopes that she would choose him. His heart had already broken once—he was not sure he could survive it breaking anew.

The serving woman ushered him through a door, down a dim hallway, and into another room at the end.

Standing about on the rug in the middle were a round dozen other men, all of them older than he, looking at each other uneasily and making no attempt at conversation. As he entered, they all turned to glare at him as if one.

These were the other suitors, then. His rivals.

He eyed them with distaste. Before the night was out, one of them would be instated as Caroline's new protector, with all the rights over her person that the position entailed. Whichever one it was, he hated him already. The man could not possibly deserve her.

None of them were Caroline's type. They were fat, for starters, and smelled of stale tobacco smoke.

Nonetheless they had the aura of superiority around them that only rich men can have. He bet none of them were self-made like him, or had even so much as done an honest day's work in their lives. Overweight, old money pratts, the lot of them.

Having dismissed the men as unworthy of his Caroline, he turned his attention to the room. The paintings on the walls were highly erotic, of men and women in various positions and poses. The overt sexuality of the room made his skin prickle with a fine sheen of sweat. He ran one finger around his collar to loosen it.

An older woman approached him from the far end, sweeping forward in her long skirts with a regal air. "Good day, Mr. Savage. I am delighted to see you were able to attend our little auction after all. If you will please give me your proposal, I shall begin the evening's activities very shortly. I believe all my expected guests have now arrived."

Dominic handed over his envelope with an inward sigh of despair. He knew right now his offer could not possibly match those of the other gentlemen in the room. Indeed, he did not even know why he had changed his mind at the last moment and decided to attend after all, except that he could not bear the idea that Caroline would walk out of his life for good without him even reaching out a single finger to stop her.

Mrs. Erskine placed his envelope along with the others on a silver tray that rested on a nearby sideboard.

Dominic stood away from the others and made no attempt to introduce himself. He was in no mood to make idle conversation with his rivals.

A young woman entered the room and walked confidently across the rug to retrieve the silver tray holding the envelopes.

Dominic's eyes followed her every movement, as did those of the other men in the room. It was the same woman who had greeted him at the door, but she was no longer dressed as a serving girl. Indeed, although fully clothed, she was barely dressed at all.

She wore a long silver dress that clung to her slim figure, revealing every curve she possessed. A plunging neckline displayed most of her bosom, while at the back a split showed off the entire length of her legs as she walked. As she left the room she gave the assembled men a shy smile before departing with the tray and his last chance to win the heart of Caroline Clemens.

There was a brief, awkward shuffling silence before Mrs. Erskine took control of the proceedings once again. "Gentlemen, I thank you for your presence here this evening. As you will surmise, Miss Clemens is now examining your offers. She will consider them as she pleases. She is under no obligation to decide on her new protector tonight, but she may well do so. Either way, she has undertaken to give us at the least a preliminary response within half an hour as to those offers she is seriously considering. Until then I have arranged for a little entertainment for you. This coffeehouse is well regarded in certain circles for the quality of our entertainment." Her last sentence was delivered with a smile and a knowing look at several of the men in the room.

Caroline stood in a small side room looking with trepidation at the papers arrayed before her. One of these would set the direction for the next few years of her life. Such a small token, and yet so packed with fate.

One of Mrs. Erskine's girls had opened the envelopes and spread the offers over a large desk, the names of the proposers hidden on the underside.

The instructions for the preparation of an offer included a clear statement that the name of the proposer was to be on the reverse side of the offer itself so that she could decide on a new protector without bias. For once in her life she wanted to make a decision based on logic and reason, not on emotion. As a true courtesan, she would take the man who offered her the best deal, whether she found him personally attractive or not. One man's money was as good as another's.

Before she examined the detail of the offers, she couldn't resist a peek into the lounge to gain an idea of what would be in store for her in the years to come.

Focusing through a small spy hole, she peered at a small group of overweight men, most of whom were enveloped in a haze of evil blue cigar smoke. And they all had faces covered in various styles of itchy whiskers.

A grim set to her mouth, she realized the prospects of a

handsome man, of a kind and strong man, even of a clean-shaven man, didn't look good.

No matter, the choice would be easier if all her prospects were equally unappealing. She would end up with a man whose best asset would be his wealth. That was all she had left to care about now.

Dominic, standing apart from the other men, watched as they turned as one man to look at the two young women who had taken up center stage on the rug. From the corner of the room another woman began to play a sensuous piece on the piano to which the other two danced.

He watched idly as they moved, their loose clothes flowing like grasses in the wind, every so often allowing a hint of nipple or a lithe leg to be exposed.

They moved together briefly, each removing a silk scarf from the other, allowing even more of their nakedness to be seen.

With his fate out of his control, Dominic had no stomach for such shallow dalliances. His mind was absorbed by the fact that Caroline was nearby, with a goodly choice of offers to consider.

And of course one dismal offer. His.

What a fool he'd been to even bother to come. What he offered, Caroline could get anywhere. There was nothing special about him.

Angrily, he turned on his heel and headed for the door.

★ ★ ★

Caroline examined the offers as they lay on the table, trying to relate each to the men in the adjacent room. Most of them were superficially similar in appearance, with densely packed script and columns of figures. It was if they had been written from the same boilerplate by the same lawyer or accountant.

One, however, caught her eye with its difference. The script was larger and untidy, with a few paragraphs and not a hint of arithmetic to be seen. She started to read.

It is not fire
But it burns the body
It is not a weapon
But it pierces the heart

It is my love for you, and it is everything I have to offer.

With a gasp, she fell back, the words like a physical blow. She did not need to read any further. None of the men she had spied in the room could have written that. She knew of only one who could have done so. Rushing back to the peephole, she peered once more into the room beyond.

It was the movement that caught her eye. Beyond the near-naked girls who danced around the leering men, a lean figure was striding to the door. Dominic! Despite the unnatural hunch to his shoulders, she would recognize his figure anywhere.

Damn logic and reason, and damn the money! Her estate

would be enough to keep both of them in comfort. And if it wasn't, well, she would rather be poor with Dominic by her side than be a wealthy woman without him.

With a rush that scattered the papers to the floor, she fled the room and down the hallway, desperate that he should not leave before she could see him.

Dominic found himself once more in the coffeehouse proper.

"A table, sir?"

With a moment's consideration he slumped into his coat. There was nothing here for him, yet there was nothing beyond the door, either. He might as well gather his strength before leaving. "Yes, a table please, and a chop and a coffee to go with it."

Sitting at the table, he picked up an old copy of *The Times*, idly perusing the financial section. His latest venture had been a success, and he was looking for a new opportunity. Not that it would do him any good, seeing as he'd left all that he most wanted behind the door he had just shut.

Caroline burst into the coffeehouse, breathless after her flight from the room and the rush down the hallway. The eating room was empty save for a man reading a newspaper, his identity hidden behind the large broadsheet.

Catching her breath, she walked slowly over to the lone diner. "I always loved to listen to your voice when you recited poetry."

She reached out, took the newspaper, and looked into the eyes of the man she loved.

Dominic felt as if he were frozen to the chair. She was there, in front of him. Caroline.

After a long moment he found his voice. "And I always loved to listen to the beating of your heart, knowing the courage that lay inside."

His own heart hammered inside his chest as he waited for what she would say next.

Caroline did not keep him waiting long. Laying one hand on top of his, she looked straight into his eyes. "I love you, Dominic," she said. "And I accept your offer."

LEDA SWANN is the writing duet of Cathy and Brent. They write out of their home overlooking the sea in peaceful New Zealand. When not writing they have busy lives working in the technology industry, bringing up four children, and enjoying an adventurous outdoor life that ranges from the mountains to the sea.

LEDA SWANN